JENNINGS
UNLIMITED

More Jennings books to watch out for:

and the new Jennings book
JENNINGS AGAIN!

Author's note

Each of the Jennings books is a story complete in itself. Apart from the title, JENNINGS GOES TO SCHOOL, the books can be read in any order, and for this reason I have chosen some of the later titles for early publication in this edition.

Anthony Buckeridge

JENNINGS UNLIMITED

Anthony Buckeridge

PAN MACMILLAN
CHILDREN'S BOOKS

for Toby Price

First published 1967 by William Collins & Sons Co. Ltd

Paperback edition with illustrations by Mays, published
1991 by MACMILLAN CHILDREN'S BOOKS
A division of Pan Macmillan Children's Books Limited
London and Basingstoke
Associated companies throughout the world

ISBN 0-333-55660-7

A CIP catalogue record for this book is available from the British Library

Phototypeset by Intype, London

Printed and bound in Great Britain by
Cox & Wyman Ltd, Reading, Berkshire

CONTENTS

Jennings Unlimited was originally published as *Jennings Abounding*. The title has been changed to *Jennings Unlimited* in order to avoid confusion with the author's musical play, *Jennings Abounding*, published by Samuel French Ltd.

LIST OF ILLUSTRATIONS

Chapter 1

French Cricket

The missile was badly aimed. It shot past its target shoulder-high, and went skimming over the banisters and down the well of the staircase . . . Two storeys below it caught Mr Wilkins a glancing blow on the right shoulder as he was coming up the stairs from the hall.

Mr Wilkins was not hurt, but his dignity was ruffled. It is rare to find a schoolmaster who enjoys being slapped on the shoulder by an off-white tennis shoe while patrolling the building in the course of his duties. He retrieved the shoe and continued on his way: as he did so, an exchange of insults between unseen adversaries rang out from the landing above.

"Rotten shot! Missed by a mile! Couldn't hit a haystack! Couldn't hit a flea," squawked the first antagonist.

"I'll bet you couldn't hit a flea, either," retorted his opponent. "Not with a mouldy old tennis shoe at twenty-five yards, anyway. And I'll tell you another thing . . ."

The master on duty had no difficulty in recognising the voices. "Jennings! . . . Darbishire! Come here!" he boomed up the stairs.

The insults ceased in mid-squawk and two slim figures appeared at the stairhead. Hurrying down to the first landing, they stood looking up at the duty master with the wide-eyed innocence of poodles hoping for a biscuit.

"Yes, sir?" said Jennings.

He was the taller of the two: a boy of eleven with restless hands, fidgeting feet and the wide-awake look of one eager to take a leading part in everything going on around him.

His companion had no such ambitions. Fair-haired and bespectacled, C. E. J. Darbishire was content to let his friend take the initiative in such out-of-school activities as took his fancy. Even so, the role of right-hand man to the impetuous Jennings was beset by hazards, and the loyal supporter often found himself in situations from which his cautious nature shrank in alarm.

Mr Wilkins switched on the special tone of disapproval which he kept for occasions of this sort. "What on earth do you boys think you're playing at?" he demanded. "You know perfectly well you're not allowed to fool about in the corridors, throwing shoes at each other."

"We weren't actually *throwing* them sir," Jennings defended himself. "Darbishire was very kindly passing me my tennis shoe when I—er—sort of dodged."

"Did you, indeed! It was bound to be *your* shoe, Jennings, that was the cause of the trouble."

Mr Wilkins was still holding the offending item of

footwear, and he glanced inside it to make sure that it was correctly marked with the owner's name. At once, his eyebrows rose in puzzled wonder: there was no name tape, but inscribed in black ink on the underside of the tongue was the word *Ditto*.

"Did you write this, Jennings?" he asked.

"Yes, sir. You told me to . . ."

"I'm quite sure I didn't do anything of the sort."

"Oh, but you *did*, sir," the boy insisted. "Last Saturday in the changing room, you said we'd all got to have our names on everything."

"And since when has your name been Ditto?"

"Oh, it isn't *really*, sir. Not in so many words, as you might say," Jennings went on. "But you see I wrote *Jennings* on one of my shoes, and when I showed you, you told me to write the same on the other one."

"Yes, but, you silly little boy . . ."

"And ditto means the same, doesn't it, sir?" added Darbishire in case the point was too subtle for the slow-witted understanding of a grown-up. "So Jennings was only carrying out your orders, really, and . . ."

"Be quiet, Darbishire," snapped Mr Wilkins. "You must need your heads examined, the pair of you. How in the name of thunder is anyone supposed to locate the owner of a shoe marked *Ditto*?"

Jennings looked surprised. "Everyone would know it was mine, sir, because nobody else thought of doing it like that," he argued. "That makes it my own special invention, copyright reserved, as you might say. So if you look at it that way . . ."

"That's enough nonsense," said Mr Wilkins. "It doesn't

make sense, *whichever* way you look at it."

That was the trouble with boys like Jennings and Darbishire, Mr Wilkins always maintained. The things they said and the things they did seemed fantastic when looked at from his point of view.

He was a kindly man at heart and fond of the boys whom he taught, but more often than not these virtues were concealed behind a testy manner and a short supply of patience. Gruffly he said, "You've no business to be fooling about indoors. You're supposed to be out on the cricket field watching the first eleven match."

"Yes, sir."

"Off you go at once, then—and take that ridiculous tennis shoe with you. And if it hasn't got your name written in it properly the next time I see you, I'll—I'll . . . Well, you'd better look out."

Jennings retrieved his ill-fated footwear, and as the boys scurried off downstairs and across the hall they could hear Mr Wilkins mumbling to himself in the background.

"Right shoe, *Jennings:* left shoe *Ditto*." he was muttering in tones of quiet despair. "Tut—tut—tut! What on earth will the silly boys be thinking of next!"

The first XI match was just about to start as Jennings and Darbishire arrived at the cricket field.

The grounds of Linbury Court School extended over several acres: in front of the main building was a tarmac playground bounded on two sides by the L-shaped block and on the third by outbuildings. From here a gravel drive led down to the main gate, skirting the playing fields and the headmaster's garden before passing through a belt of rough grass and woodland that lay beyond.

Apart from the first XI busying themselves in and around the cricket pavilion, the remainder of the seventy-nine boarders of Linbury Court were settling down to watch the match against the neighbouring school of Bracebridge.

This was a pastime that normally kept the juniors quiet for the first half hour of the game. After that, their interest tended to flag, and watching the match gave place to staging crawling contests for caterpillars and stuffing handfuls of grass down neighbours' necks. In order to rivet their minds on the game for as long as possible the boys were encouraged to keep the score, and with this in view most of the younger spectators had brought home-made scoring pads, and roughly a quarter of them had remembered to bring pencils as well.

Jennings and Darbishire found a place on the bank beside Temple, a sturdy, square-rigged third-former, and his friend Venables, an untidy eleven-year-old with perpetually trailing shoe-laces and untucked shirt. Venables had brought a toy telescope with him to follow the finer points of the game in close up, and Temple was clutching his camera ready to record the highlights for posterity.

"You can take a photo of me if you like," said Jennings as he sat down. He pulled the corners of his eyes and stretched his mouth into a hideous grimace which left the photographer unmoved.

"Not with this camera, I couldn't," Temple objected. "I'd need a special wide-angled lens to get both your ears in."

Seated close at hand was Henri Dufour, a French boy who had arrived as a boarder at the beginning of the term. It was partly due to a chance meeting with Jennings and Darbishire that had prompted Monsieur Dufour to send his son to Linbury* and for this reason the two friends felt it was their special duty to help their French colleague to find his feet in an alien land.

At the beginning of the summer term Henri's knowledge of English had been slight, and during his first bewildered days he had despaired of ever being able to communicate with the jabbering companions whose ceaseless chatter bounced off his eardrums without meaning. But, as the weeks passed, the sounds began to make sense and now, after two months of striving to make himself understood—and shouting to make himself heard—he had, by trial and error, attained a fair standard of spoken English.

Jennings glanced at Darbishire and said, "I reckon it's time we taught Henri a bit more about cricket. He still hasn't a clue about the proper names of things."

"Leave it to me. I'll straighten him out," Darbishire volunteered. His eyes brightened behind his dust-splattered glasses, for the role of tutor made him feel important. "I'm better at explaining things than you."

Though he had made good progress in other directions, the laws of cricket were a closed book to Henri Dufour. He took part in junior practice games several times each week, running whenever someone told him to run: and, when fielding, he dutifully threw the ball at the head of whichever member of his side was shouting the loudest.

* See *Especially Jennings*

But he had no clear idea of what the running and the throwing were all about, and he was delighted when Darbishire squeezed in beside him on the bank and offered to take his sporting education in hand.

"I'll sit here and explain everything that happens," the tutor assured him. "Don't be afraid to ask me if there's anything you don't understand."

Venables, two places away, ceased inspecting the pitch through his telescope and hooted with laughter.

"Hark who's talking! Listen to the expert," he jeered. "Don't you believe a word he tells you, Henri. Old Darbi's cricket is pathetic. He plays like a flat-footed newt."

"You don't have to be an expert player to explain the rules," Darbishire retorted. He was annoyed with Venables for drawing attention to an undeniable fact: Darbishire's cricket *was* pathetic, but he strove to make up for his shortcomings by concentrating on the theory of the game. "And anyway, Mr Carter wouldn't have appointed me reserve third XI scorer if I didn't know the rules, so three boos to you!"

Venables grinned. "We'll help you out if you get stuck," he offered.

The umpires were already in their places, and Mr Carter, the senior assistant master, was standing at the bowling end as the home side emerged from the pavilion to take the field.

"Well, now, that bit of short grass where Mr Carter's standing is called the pitch," Darbishire began.

"Ze peach," echoed Henri solemnly.

"Ah, but not always," Venables broke in. "It's called the wicket, too."

"Ze wicked," repeated Henri.

"Yes. For instance, you can have a batsman's wicket or a bowler's wicket or even a sticky wicket and it still means the pitch," Venables maintained.

"Never mind about that now," Darbishire said curtly. If Venables was going to quibble about shades of meaning they'd never get anywhere. "Now, Henri, you see those three sticks of wood where Mr Carter is standing? They're called the stumps."

"And Mr Carter is the stumpire, no?" Henri deduced brightly.

"No, you're mixing up *ump* and *stump*. It's the three sticks at each end that are known as the stumps."

"Ah, but not always," Venables broke in again. "The stumps are called the wicket too, don't forget. How about leg before *wicket*! How about *wicket*-keeper!"

Darbishire was furious. He turned on the interrupter and squawked, "Who's teaching him—you or me? And anyway you're wrong because you don't draw *wickets* at the end of the match—you draw *stumps*."

"That's got nothing to do with it," retorted Venables. "And anyway, what about . . ."

The tutor shut his ears to the interruptions and turned back to his pupil. "Now the bowler bowls to the batsman, although according to the rules he's not really the batsman—he's the striker. And the bloke the other end is the wicket-keeper. He can stump you if you're out of your crease. It's quite simple, really. Just watch and see what happens."

The pupil was baffled. So far as he could understand the pitch meant the wicket and the wicket meant the stumps. Surely, then, the pitch and the stumps must be the same thing!

By this time the game was under way, and shortly afterwards the first wicket fell when the Bracebridge score had just reached double figures. The opening batsman, playing too far forward to a good-length delivery, missed the ball completely and was out of ground when the bails were whipped off behind him.

As the clapping died away Darbishire decided to test his pupil's progress. "How was he out?" he asked.

Henri was all smiles. "He was wicketed by the stump-keeper," he cried triumphantly.

As they waited for the next batsman, a high-flying pigeon swept across the playing field, soaring over the heads of the spectators to swoop down and land on a top-floor window-sill of the main school building.

Jennings leapt to his feet and followed the bird's flight with obvious excitement. "There it is again, Darbi! It's the same one," he shrilled.

Darbishire immediately forgot his pupil and jumped up. "Where? Where? Are you sure?"

"Of course I'm sure. It's just touched down in the usual place."

"What's all the panic about?" demanded Temple.

"It's a pigeon we've been watching," Jennings informed him. "Either it's got lost or it's having an extra long rest, because it's been roosting on the attic window-ledge for nearly a week now. Darbi and I have been keeping tabs on it."

Temple was unable to see anything unusual in such an occurrence. "So what! There's a whole colony of them in the wood by the pond. Surely they can fly where they like without asking your permission."

"Ah, but this isn't just an ordinary old wood-pigeon—you can tell by the shape. It's a carrier-pigeon and it's probably got a message on its leg, if you could get close enough to have a proper look."

"What sort of message?" Temple demanded suspiciously.

"How should I know? Might even be a top security secret."

Venables laughed derisively. "What, on a pigeon? Do me a favour!" With mock seriousness he added, "They've got a different way of doing it now, you know: it's called radio. Maybe you haven't heard of it."

"Don't be funny," snorted Jennings. "For all you know they may still use pigeons for—er—well, special cases, for instance."

"Such as what? Messages from the moon? Of course, if this famous pigeon of yours is wearing a space-helmet we'll know its . . ."

"Shut up and pass me your feeble old spy-glass. I may be able to see if it's got something tied to its leg." So saying, Jennings snatched up the toy telescope and trained it on the distant window-sill. The range was too great for the instrument to be of the slightest use, but he was reluctant to admit defeat, and was still straining his eyes on the target when the duty master strolled by to make sure that the boys were concentrating on the game with the close attention that the headmaster expected of them.

"Jennings! What are you doing?"

The boy swung round with a start of surprise. "Watching the match, sir."

"With your back to the pitch?"

"Well, just at that moment I wasn't looking, sir. I was—er—bird-watching."

"Bird-watching! During a cricket match!" Mr Wilkins was horrified.

"Not exactly bird-watching, sir. Pigeon-spotting, really. You see I've got a theory that this pigeon is a . . ."

But Mr Wilkins wasn't interested in ornithological theories. It was less than half an hour since he had had occasion to reprimand Jennings and here was the boy again indulging in senseless behaviour. "If you can't conduct yourself like a civilised human being, you don't deserve the same privileges as other people," he said severely. "Go indoors and sit at your desk until the others come in for swimming."

"Yes, sir."

It was no great hardship to be sent indoors, for, according to the afternoon's arrangements all the junior spectators would be coming in from the cricket field during the tea interval to get ready for the daily swimming session in the school pool. Jennings was aware of this and unwisely permitted the ghost of a smile to crease his lips when the punishment was imposed.

Mr Wilkins saw the smile and was furious. "Insolence!" he barked. "Right! You can miss your swimming today, as well."

"Oh, but sir!" Jennings protested. The punishment was no longer lenient: he had been looking forward to swimming.

"You heard what I said." The duty master pointed to the grey stone building with the stem of his pipe. "Indoors at once!" He waited until the boy had disappeared round the corner of the pavilion and then sat down on the bank to watch the game for a couple of overs.

Chapter 2

Feathered Guest

Ten yards away and just out of earshot, Darbishire resumed his interrupted lecture.

"Well, now, Henri, the bloke who's batting now is the one we call first wicket down. And so it goes on till the last man—that's batsman number eleven—goes in ninth wicket. And the one who's not out when everybody's been in 'carries his bat' as they say. D'you follow?"

The pupil was out of his depth trying to fit eleven men into nine batting places. And the idea of only one batsman carrying his bat was ridiculous. They *all* carried bats when it was their turn for an innings, Was Darbishire making fun of him, he wondered?

"You mock me," he said accusingly.

"No, honestly! You don't understand. Look, I'll try and explain it in French." Darbishire frowned as he wrestled with the problem of translation. He decided to say: *If you are not out you carry your bat*, but a French equivalent for the last word eluded him. He turned towards Mr Wilkins, still seated nearby, and called aloud, "Sir, please sir, Mr Wilkins, sir. What's the French for a bat?"

"*Une chauve-souris*," Mr Wilkins replied absently, his mind still on Jennings' bird-watching and pigeon-spotting exploits.

"Thank you, sir." With confidence the linguist turned back to his pupil. "*Si vous n'êtes pas dehors, vous portez votre chauve-souris.*"

Henri shrugged helplessly. Was there no limit to the lunatic laws of this incredible game! He knew what a cricket bat was: he used one every time he played. So why confuse the issue by talking about the mouse-like creatures that flutter overhead in the dusk? It didn't make sense.

He consoled himself with the thought that next term they would be playing football: and that was a game with rules that *everybody* could understand!

In through the side door, past the shoe-lockers, across the hall and up the stairs to Form Three classroom . . .

Jennings paused in the doorway: Mr Wilkins had said that he was to sit at his desk until junior swimming was over. But surely there would be no harm in first paying a brief visit to the attic for a possible glimpse of the pigeon at close quarters! It would have to be a secret visit, for the attic was out of bounds; but as everyone (including Mr Wilkins) was out on the games field, there wasn't much risk of being caught!

Jennings turned back along the corridor, heading for

the narrow staircase at the far end of the building. Here, too, he was in forbidden territory or, at best, in that part of the school which the boys had no reason to visit.

As he reached the foot of the staircase he heard the patter of descending feet round the bend beyond the half landing. He stopped short. Was it Matron, perhaps? Or Robinson, the school caretaker? Whoever it was, Jennings had no wish for an encounter.

Retreat was out of the question, for the corridor stretched away behind him with no form of cover. The only hope of concealment lay in a wicker laundry hamper, standing empty with the lid thrown back.

The hamper was under the window in a recess, a yard from where Jennings was standing. Quickly he climbed inside, crouched down and tugged at the lid which dropped with a slight thud and tinkle as the hasp fell into place on the rim. It was dark inside but not completely so, for a glimmer of light filtered through the loose weave of the wicker-work.

For some seconds Jennings knelt there, hardly daring to breathe, while the footsteps descended the stairs ... They were light footsteps: not Robinson, not a master he decided. Obviously Matron, or one of the domestic staff. He would be quite safe if he made no sound until she had gone past.

The footsteps drew level, passed by and appeared to be receding when—so far as Jennings could judge—they turned in their tracks and came back and stopped beside the basket.

Tense with foreboding he awaited the raising of the lid, the startled gasp as Matron, clutching an armful of dirty linen, peered down into a hamper which she had every reason to believe was empty.

Oddly enough, this didn't happen. Instead, the wicker-work creaked under the strain of someone first kneeling and then standing upright on the lid. There came the shuffling of feet setting themselves at ease, and then a long silence broken only by occasional fidgeting and shifting of position.

Time passed, but nothing more occurred. Jennings was thunderstruck. What on earth was Matron playing at! Little though he knew of the habits of school Matrons, it seemed strange to him that members of the nursing profession should choose to spend their free time perched on rickety laundry baskets in draughty corridors. Had the strain of coping with the health problems of seventy-nine boarders deranged the woman's mind?

At that moment the hamper rocked and the lid sagged as the unseen feet broke into an improvised dance and a shrill voice was raised in applause. "Hooray! Good shot! Wow! Boundary four!"

Neither the voice not the idiom belonged to Matron. With a start of surprise the prisoner in the basket recognised the gleeful tones of Atkinson, a fair-haired excitable colleague in Form Three.

"Hey!" Jennings shouted.

The effect was dramatic. Startled by the ventriloquial shout from nowhere, Atkinson jumped down from his perch and scurried away along the corridor. As he did so, Jennings tried to open the lid of the hamper but to his dismay it refused to yield. Thinking back, he remembered hearing the hasp fall into place over the staple when he had shut himself in.

"Hey Atkinson! Stop! Come back! Help!" Jennings yelled at the top of his voice.

In the distance the scurrying footsteps skidded to a halt. Then a nervous voice called, "Who's that in there?"

"It's me. Jennings. I can't get out."

"Why can't you get out? What are you doing?"

"Never mind what I'm doing. Come and open the lid."

The footsteps returned, fingers fumbled with the fastening and the lid was flung back. Atkinson stared down at Jennings in bewilderment.

"What on earth did you want to shut yourself in there for?" he demanded.

"I didn't *want* to. It was an accident," Jennings explained. "I thought you were Matron."

"Why? do I look like Matron?"

"No, not really. Only I heard footsteps. What did you run away for when I called out?"

"I thought you were Matron."

"That's crazy. We couldn't *both* be Matron," Jennings pointed out.

"Well, you know what I mean," Atkinson said vaguely. "There I was looking out of the window when this voice boomed out from outer space or somewhere. How was I to know who it was?"

Jennings climbed out of the hamper. "I was on my way up to the little attic. You can come with me if you like."

"You won't be able to get in. The door's locked," Atkinson informed him. "I was just coming down from there."

By way of reply Jennings took a key from his pocket. "My tuck-box key," he announced. "I happen to know it opens the attic because last term Darbi and I went round trying it on every door in the school when we were looking for a secret hide-out."

On the way to the top floor Atkinson explained the reasons for his unusual behaviour. Owing to a cold from which he was recovering, Matron had forbidden him to go out of doors. Anxious to watch the match, he had been wandering round the upper storeys of the building trying to decide which window commanded the best view of the pitch.

"I could see quite well from that laundry basket until you put the wind up me, bellowing like a foghorn," he complained. "You can't blame me for beetling off, seeing that I was out of bounds, anyway."

By this time they had reached the top floor and were making their way along a passage with doors on either side leading into attics and storage rooms. At the end of the passage was a door, smaller than the others. Here they stopped and Jennings produced his key.

"This is a fantastically secret mission I'd have you know." He paused in the act of unlocking the door. "You've got to keep dead quiet when I open up, or you'll scare it away."

Atkinson's eyes opened wide. "Scare what?"

"There's a pigeon on the window-ledge—at least there *was*," Jennings explained. "My theory is that it's got a secret message tied to its leg, but if you go barging in shouting your head off like a bull on a bicycle we shan't have a hope."

He opened the door and the two boys tiptoed inside.

The little attic tucked away under the eaves was hardly more than a large cupboard with a window. Its main function was to house the cold water tank standing in one corner, from which a maze of pipes criss-crossed about the room before disappearing through the floorboards.

Outside on the window-sill was the pigeon.

"Any message?" Atkinson breathed hopefully.

"I can't see its legs—it's sitting on them," Jennings whispered. "We'll have to find out how tame it is first."

Still on tiptoe he crossed to the window and fumbled with the catch. The pigeon watched him with head cocked and made no attempt to fly away. With extreme care Jennings raised the sash. Still the bird remained motionless, but when he stretched out a hand towards it, it retreated under the eaves well out of reach. Here it settled and continued to watch him with one cautious eye.

Jennings withdrew his arm and turned to his companion. "It's a bit suspicious, but it'll be quite tame when it gets to know us," he surmised. "The first thing to do is to make friends with it."

To Atkinson, friendship and food were closely related. "I'll get it something to eat," he offered. "I've got some stuff in my tuck-box."

"Your tuck-box!" Jennings clicked his teeth in reproach. "It won't touch liquorice allsorts and jelly-babies, you know. Pigeons eat peas and beans and things."

"I've got a tin of *baked* beans," Atkinson said doubtfully. "They might be all right if I washed the tomato sauce off."

Jennings was scornful. "You'll be expecting him to eat them on toast next, I shouldn't wonder," he snorted.

Their best plan, he decided, would be to explain their needs to Mrs Hackett who came in daily from Linbury village to work in the school kitchen. As one who had access to the stock of beans, lentils, porridge oats and dried peas which the school larder must surely contain, her co-operation would be invaluable.

"You go and ask her," Jennings commanded. "I'll stay here and keep an eye on him so he'll get used to me."

Atkinson was away on his errand for a long time. For the first few minutes Jennings leant out of the window making coo-ing noises designed to instil confidence in his feathered friend, but as these had no effect he withdrew his head and glanced round the room seeking some way of spending the time of waiting. Somebody, at some unknown period of time, had left a large box of drawing pins on the low wooden beam that traversed the room. For want of better employment Jennings took the lid off the box and began to inscribe his name by sticking the brass-headed pins into the beam just above his head.

First he made a large J using a dozen pins set close together in a wide cross-piece and a further dozen for the vertical stroke and the final curve. Then he printed a smaller ENNINGS six inches high and spreading a yard or more along the beam.

He stood back to admire his handiwork and accidentally kicked over the cardboard box, scattering the remaining pins across the floor.

It was a long time since the attic had been swept, and by the time he had squeezed behind the cold water tank to retrieve a handful of drawing pins Jennings' head and ears were covered with a pall of dust and a network of webs. He was just wiping the shroud out of his eyes when the messenger returned bearing a small paper bag.

"Still here, is he?" Atkinson demanded. "Goodo! It took me ages to find Mrs Hackett, and then she tried to make out that they only ate worms and things!"

"Didn't she give you anything?"

"Oh, yes." Atkinson opened the bag which contained a mixed assortment of bread, toast crusts, raw peas and sprout tops. Whether this was suitable fare remained to be seen, so Jennings emptied the bag on to the sill and retired to a safe distance.

The bird watched him but made no attempt to inspect the food at close quarters.

"He'll eat all right as soon as he gets to know us," Jennings decided. "We could start a group of pigeon wardens to take turns in feeding him."

"Bags I be one," said Atkinson. "Just you and me, eh!"

"And Darbi," Jennings said firmly. It would be unthinkable to take part in a project from which his best friend was excluded.

He glanced at his watch: it was later than he had thought. By now the junior spectators would have left the cricket field and be splashing in the swimming pool.

"Come on! Time we weren't here!" Jennings bundled Atkinson out into the passage and followed at his heels. Turning in the doorway he took a last glimpse at the pigeon on the window-sill, and as he did so the bird stood up and strutted a few paces forward to inspect the crumbly offerings laid out for its refreshment. Jennings gave his companion a friendly punch in the ribs.

"I was right. It *is* a carrier," he crowed. "I caught sight of its leg just then, and it's got a ring on it."

Chapter 3

The Writing on the Wall

The swimmers had returned from the pool when the boys arrived downstairs, and this meant that Jennings' period of detention in the classroom was automatically over. Either his absence had been noticed or it had not: in any case it was now too late to do anything except hope that Mr Wilkins had forgotten all about him.

It was nearly time for tea. Atkinson wandered away to the common-room and Jennings made for the wash-basins to tidy himself for the meal. Here he found Darbishire who paused in the act of wringing out his swimming trunks to comment upon his friend's appearance.

"Wow! What on earth have you been doing, Jen? You look like a dirty grey ghost."

"We've been up in the tank attic, Atki and me, keeping tabs on the pigeon," Jennings explained. "It's a special, secret-message-carrier all right, and you've been elected to a special, secret committee to help feed it."

"Terrific!" approved the secret committee-man. "You'd better wash your face and hands before you go in to tea, though. Old Wilkie will go into orbit if he sees you like that."

Jennings filled the adjoining wash-basin with cold water and ducked his head beneath the surface. "How did the match go?" he asked, as he massaged his scalp with his fingers.

"They're still playing. They'd made seventy-something for six when Mr Hind brought us in for swimming." Darbishire sighed and shook his head. "Poor old Henri! He still hasn't got a clue. I tried to explain about bowling a maiden over and he thought I meant knocking a young girl down."

Jennings raised his dripping head from the basin. "Did he really!"

"Well, no, actually I made that up," Darbishire confessed with a giggle. "But it's the sort of thing he *would* think, isn't it?'

In the distance the tea-bell rang. Jennings rubbed his head on a roller-towel and, with his hair still damp, hurried along to the dining-hall for the evening meal.

From a rostrum at one end of the dining-hall, Mr Wilkins looked down at the rows of champing jaws, alert for any sign of slovenly table manners or voices raised above the level permitted for polite conversation.

He could find no cause for complaint: nobody was slouching in his seat or demanding the bread and butter at a volume of eighty-five decibels. All was well—except perhaps at the third-form table where Jennings was entertaining his friends with an impromptu mime of a man who had just bitten an exceptionally hot potato.

Ah, yes, Jennings! The duty master narrowed his gaze and frowned with rising suspicion. Since sending him indoors earlier in the afternoon, he had not given Jennings another thought. But now there was evidence to suggest that, far from carrying out Mr Wilkins' orders, the culprit had flouted them in the most flagrant fashion. The little handbell on the master's table rang out and the room fell silent.

"A word with you, Jennings," Mr Wilkins began, and the boy rose to his feet. "I was under the impression that I forbade you to go swimming this afternoon with the rest of the junior school."

"Yes, sir," Jennings agreed.

"Then why did you disobey my orders and go into the pool?"

Jennings was shocked by the charge. "Oh, but I didn't sir. Honestly, I never went near it."

"Indeed!" Mr Wilkins glanced round the room to make sure that everyone was listening before he played his trump card. "Very well, then, Jennings, if you did *not* go into the swimming bath, do you mind telling me why your hair is *still damp*!"

"Yes, sir. I put my head in the wash-basin just before tea."

There was a burst of laughter from all over the room. Unaware of the real reason for the hasty shampoo, it was natural for the boys (and for Mr Wilkins, too) to assume that this had been a ruse to make the master jump to the wrong conclusion.

Mr Wilkins quelled the laughter with a glance. "Are you trying to be funny, boy!" he demanded.

"No, honestly, sir."

The room was hushed waiting to see how the master would react to the alleged attempt to take advantage of him. Mr Wilkins sensed the atmosphere and wisely lowered the temperature of his wrath. It would be better to treat the whole thing as a feeble joke rather than turn a mole-hill into a mountain.

In a quiet, almost indulgent voice he said, "You'd better watch your step, Jennings, my lad, or you'll be finding yourself in *real* trouble before the term's much older."

During the next few days Jennings spent most of his free time in the tank attic, trying to win the confidence of the bird on the window-sill. The task was not easy, for his journeys to the top storey had to be undertaken with a wary eye on the movements of the master on duty. And as the pigeon showed no sign of responding to his cooing invitations he was unable to get close enough to examine the ring on its right leg.

Atkinson and Darbishire, enrolled as assistant pigeon-feeders, had no more success: the bird resisted all attempts to lure it within arm's length and did little more than peck at the food provided for its refreshment.

"We can't go on like this. We're bound to get caught before we catch the pigeon," Jennings said to his fellow bird-fanciers after tea on Thursday evening. "If we don't have any luck by the end of the week, I vote we call the whole thing off and let him look after himself."

Darbishire wrinkled his nose and said, "I reckon it's

this grotty old school food we're putting out for him. You can't expect racing pigeons to put up with the mouldy sort of stuff that *we* have to make do with. If only we could get hold of some genuine pigeon mixture, we'd be laughing."

"Why not ask Mrs Hackett?" Atkinson suggested. "She lives just across the road from the village stores and they're bound to sell bird seed and stuff there."

So this was decided upon. Mrs Hackett, when approached (and sworn to secrecy), was quite willing to purchase some suitable fare from the corn-chandling counter of the Linbury General Stores and Post Office. On Friday, she arrived with small packets of maple peas, wheat, maize, millet and linseed which she had been assured were ideal for the purpose.

Jennings was delighted. During morning break he paid a furtive visit to the attic and sprinkled a handful of the new diet on the window-sill beside the honey-pot of drinking water which he dutifully changed every day.

By evening the handful of meal was gone, and though the bird refused to approach within arm's length of its hosts, it appeared to be far less suspicious than it had been on previous occasions.

The following day—a half-holiday—House cricket matches had been arranged between the various Houses into which the school was divided.

Jennings, who was a fair cricketer, was captain of the Drake House junior second XI, and Darbishire—who was no sort of cricketer at all—was appointed official scorer.

As it happened, Darbishire found himself the scorer for both sides, for the rival Raleigh juniors were so pressed for players to make up their team that they were unable to spare one of their number to look after the records.

"Don't worry, I can manage," Darbishire assured the teams as they foregathered at the junior's end of the playing field after lunch on Saturday. "I'll get it all down in my best writing and you Raleigh lot can copy it out into your own book after the game."

In theory, this solved the problem: in practice, it led to such chaos and confusion that the House match remained a bone of contention for some weeks to come.

Jennings won the toss and decided to bat. As he announced his decision, Darbishire sat down on a bench and opened the scoring book on his knee.

"Hey, don't all crowd round!" he protested as the Drake team jumped up on the bench and surged about him to find out the batting order. "How d'you think I can write with you mob breathing down my neck like a . . . Wow!"

His words ceased as the bench went up like a seesaw under the weight of the clamouring cricketers who collapsed in a sprawling heap with the scorer on top of the pile.

As they were struggling to their feet, Mr Carter strolled up on his way to umpire the first XI game at the other end of the playing field. The senior master was a friendly man of early middle age who was liked and respected by all the boys. Unlike his colleague Mr Wilkins, he had a shrewd understanding of the workings of the youthful mind and was never surprised by the antics of the rising generation. Even so, a cricket match starting off with a rugger scrum was a matter that called for his attention.

"What's going on here!" the master demanded. "Surely you boys can get the game started without all this fooling about."

"We weren't fooling about, sir—we had an accident," Jennings explained. "You see, Darbishire's going to score for both sides only he can't get on with it because everyone keeps pushing, sir."

"In that case we'll isolate Darbishire in the scoring-box and no one is to go anywhere near him," Mr Carter ordered.

"Coo, thanks very much, sir," said Darbishire. He was delighted at the chance of carrying out his duties from this privileged position, for the scorer's box, a wooden hut some distance along the boundary line from the bank where the teams had foregathered, was normally used only for official matches.

Mr Carter glanced at his watch. His own game was due to start and he knew that Mr Hind, the music master, was scheduled to take charge of the junior House match. So far there was no sign of him, but if Mr Hind was late that was no reason to postpone the start of the junior game.

"Off you go then, Darbishire," the master said. "There's a chance we may get a slightly more accurate record if there's no one blocking your view and shouting down your ear while you're trying to keep the score."

Mr Carter moved on; and as soon as the Drake batting order had been announced, Darbishire trotted off to record the game from his secluded vantage point.

In design, the scorer's box was shaped like a refreshment kiosk. When in use, a hinged wooden flap, extending the width of the front, was raised to roof-level where it jutted out to shield the occupants from the rays of the sun.

Darbishire was struck by this kiosk-like resemblance when he opened the flap and stood looking out at the cricket pitch bathed in the afternoon sunshine. A scrap of blackboard chalk on the ledge before him caught his eye as he laid down his scoring book; and with the idea of amusing his friends at some later stage of the afternoon he set about chalking up notices to strengthen the resemblance still further.

Lemonade—30p a bottle, he wrote on the back wall in sprawling capitals. *Ham rolls—45p each ... Crisps—20p per packet ... Ices ... Pots of Tea for the Beach ... Frying Tonight!*

He was in the middle of chalking a notice offering a discount for cash with each saucer of jellied eels, when Mr Wilkins' voice rang out in indignant protest from the playing field behind him.

"Darbishire!"

Startled, the boy swung round to see the master's head and shoulders framed in the front aperture of the hut like some prospective customer intent on buying a packet of crisps. But from the expression on his face, it was clear that he was in no mood to enter into games of make-believe and cavort with mirth at the idea of phantom ham rolls or imaginary pots of tea.

"What in the name of thunder are you doing?"

Darbishire wriggled with embarrassment. What he had *really* been doing was offering a discount for cash with non-existent saucers of sea-food, but it would be useless trying to explain this to an irate adult who couldn't be expected to see the joke. "Nothing, sir," he mumbled.

"What in the name of thunder do you think you're doing, Darbishire?" roared Mr. Wilkins

Mr Wilkins ran his eye over the chalked inscriptions and simmered with exasperation. "You must be off your head, boy," he stormed. "Supposing the headmaster were to show important visitors round the school this afternoon! What would they think if they saw *Frying Tonight* plastered all over the cricket scoring-box! Go indoors and get a wet cloth and rub this ridiculous nonsense off the walls at once."

"But, sir, I *can't* go now. I'm scoring for the junior House match and . . ."

"Don't argue with me, boy. If this puerile scribble hasn't been cleaned off in five minutes time, I'll—I'll—well, it *had* better be."

"But sir, there's no one else to . . ."

"You heard what I said," Mr Wilkins roared in a voice like a loudhailer. "At once, boy! At once!"

Darbishire darted out of the scorer's box in search of a wet cloth. As he ran he glanced back at the playing field. Jennings and Pettigrew, opening the innings for Drake, were buckling on their pads, and the opposing Raleigh side had not yet taken up their places in the field. If he ran very fast, Darbishire decided, there was a chance that he could reach the wash-room, soak a towel in a basin and be back at his post before the first ball was bowled.

But Darbishire never even reached the wash-room. As he hurtled in through the side door of the building Mr Pemberton-Oakes, the headmaster, was emerging from the school kitchen.

"Ah, Darbishire! A little job for you," the headmaster began pleasantly. "The housekeeper tells me that they're extremely short-staffed this afternoon and she would appreciate a little help in laying up the tables for tea."

Darbishire skidded to a stop and hopped from foot to foot in indecision. "Oh, but sir, I'm scoring for the junior House match and Mr Wilkins said . . ."

"Ah, yes, of course! The junior House match! Splendid!" Mr Pemberton-Oakes nodded in complete misunderstanding. "However, I have no doubt that one of your colleagues will attend to your—ah—onerous duties until you return. You will find Miss Matthews in the dining-hall." As he turned away he added with what was meant to be a roguish gleam in his eye, "Who knows, Darbishire! Miss Matthews may even feel it incumbent upon her to reward you for services rendered with a portion of her celebrated ice-cream."

"But, sir . . ."

It was useless! The headmaster was already moving away down the corridor—a remote and unapproachable figure so far as inky-fingered third-formers were concerned.

Darbishire flipped his fingers in exasperation. He would certainly be in trouble with the junior House teams for being absent from his post; furthermore he would be in trouble with Mr Wilkins for not hurrying back to wash the inscriptions off the wall. But the Head was senior to Mr Wilkins, so *his* orders would have to be obeyed first.

Low in spirit, Darbishire turned and trudged off to the dining-hall to lend Miss Matthews a hand with her housekeeping problems.

Chapter 4

Off the Record

There was still no sign of Mr Hind when the Raleigh players trotted out to take the field. Accordingly, the rival captains conferred and after some argument appointed two umpires from the batting side to take charge of the game until the master arrived.

Bromwich and Martin-Jones, both low down in the Drake batting order, were chosen for this important task. Neither of them wanted to umpire as this would interfere with their freedom to play French cricket or practise Karate while waiting for their innings. But their objections were overruled and eventually the junior House match started in earnest.

Jennings and Pettigrew, a day boy, opened the innings for Drake. The bowling was erratic and, as the first few balls were all loose long-hops on the leg, Jennings struck out at the third delivery and smote the ball to the boundary for four.

Bromwich signalled the boundary with a vague wave like a hitch-hiker thumbing a lift, but it never occurred to him to check whether the signal had been acknowledged from the scorer's box.

Then came two balls which the batsman treated with more respect, but the next one was an easy one and yielded two runs.

"Six runs in the first over. Not bad, eh!" Jennings observed to Martin-Jones as they stood together at the bowler's end at the start of the second over.

"So what! Their bowling's pathetic, anyway." Martin-Jones was still feeling resentful at being called upon to umpire in what he considered to be his free time. "Anyone could clout old Venables for four when he sends down feeble old donkey-droppers like that. It'll be time to start swanking when you've made about fifty."

Martin-Jones' criticism of the fielding side was probably justified. Owing to illness among the seniors, two players from the Raleigh second XI had been promoted to the first team and their departure had depleted the bowling strength of the junior side. As a result, the opening overs produced more than the average number of long-hops, full pitchers and near-wides, and the Drake opening pair were able to score freely on both sides of the wicket.

It had for a long while been Jennings' ambition to make fifty runs in a House match. A score of this size was seldom achieved by any player in the junior teams, and, had the opposing side been at full strength, Jennings would have been hard put to it to have made half this total.

But now his chance had come, and he hit out at the

loose bowling to such effect that in little more than half an hour the opening pair made over sixty runs, of which Jennings personally contributed forty-seven. He knew he had made exactly forty-seven because he had a habit of keeping his own score in his head all the time he was batting.

Several times the fielding side changed their bowlers in an effort to break up the first-wicket stand, but without success. Then Thompson was brought on—a bowler so lacking in skill that his friends usually measured his success by the number of deliveries which were not actually disqualified as 'wides'.

Thompson's first ball was such an inviting slow lob that Jennings walked three paces towards point and knocked it to the boundary.

Fifty one! He'd got his half century! He was so elated that he pushed the next ball he received through the slips and started to run without really looking to see just how far it had travelled.

"Come on!" he shouted as he raced down the pitch.

"No! Get back! Get back!" yelled Pettigrew from the bowler's end.

Jennings glanced over his shoulder and saw Temple in the act of throwing the ball to the wicket-keeper, so he slewed round in his tracks and hurtled back towards his crease. He was an inch short of the line when the bails were whipped off and the appeal rang out. Bromwich, umpiring at square-leg, raised his forefinger in judgment . . . He was out!

Jennings marched back to join his team-mates beaming with a sense of duty nobly done.

"I got my fifty. Fifty-one, actually," he informed his applauding colleagues. "I reckon we've got Raleigh on the trot this time."

"Old Pettigrew isn't doing too badly either," said Atkinson. "What's our first wicket total?" He glanced towards the scoring-box some distance away. "Old Darbi must have gone to sleep. He hasn't been putting the numbers up on the telly-wag board."

"Give him a chance. He can't work the telegraph *and* do the score book single-handed," Jennings pointed out. "I'll beetle over and find out how we're getting on."

Atkinson paused in the act of buckling on a pad. "Mr Carter said no one was to go over there."

"Ah, but I'm the captain. Surely *I'm* allowed to know how my own side's doing."

So saying, Jennings trotted off on his hundred-yard journey. In a matter of moments he came rushing back wide-eyed with woe and waving his arms like semaphore flags.

"Stop the game! Stop the game! Emergency!" he shouted at the top of his voice. "There's been a catastrophe. There's nobody in the scoring-box."

His tone was so urgent that the Raleigh team came hurrying from the field to see what was afoot, while the Drake players surged round their captain to hear the hideous details.

"Sabotage! That's what it is," Jennings went on with rising indignation. "Somebody wanted to stop my fifty from going down in the records so they kidnapped Darbishire to make sure of it!"

"You're bonkers! If Darbi's not there it's because he's

sloped off on his own accord," Temple argued. "The only thing we can do is to start scoring from now."

"But it's not fair. I've had my innings already. I made fifty-one," Jennings insisted.

"That's your bad luck. You can't prove it, so it won't count," said Venables. "And anyway, if it was *your* score Old Darbi was supposed to be keeping, it was up to you to make sure he was doing it."

For some minutes the argument raged round the question of why nobody noticed that Darbishire was absent from his post. The batting side maintained that they couldn't possibly have known because Mr Carter had forbidden them to go anywhere near the place in question. Those on the field, including the batsmen, excused themselves on the ground that they were far too intent on the game to observe that anything was amiss on the far side of the boundary line.

"What about the umpires, then?" Atkinson turned accusingly on Bromwich and Martin-Jones. "Why didn't you see he wasn't there?"

"I'd got the sun in my eyes," Martin-Jones defended himself.

"Huh! Feeble excuse!"

"It's right, honestly. You ask Bromwich. When the sun's behind the scorer's box, you can't see into it from out there on the pitch."

Bromwich nodded in agreement. "It's like looking into a tunnel. You just have to hope he's seen your signals."

At this point in the proceedings Mr Hind arrived to take charge of the game. For the previous half-hour he had been giving a violin lesson in the music room, and it was not until his pupil had departed that he remembered that he had offered to look after the junior House match.

Mr Hind was a tall, pale young man with a drawling voice. "What's going on here?" he inquired calmly as he meandered into the mob of arguing cricketers. "Why aren't you getting on with the game instead of squawking your heads off like a bunch of morons?"

"It's Darbishire, sir," Jennings informed him. "We all thought he was scoring, and I made fifty-one and now there's nothing to show for it."

"We've only got *your* word for it," Venables argued. "You might just as well say you made a hundred. We can't prove anything and neither can you."

The only thing to do, Mr Hind decided when he had ascertained the facts, was to appoint another scorer and start the match all over again.

Jennings was incensed. "Oh, but, sir, that's not fair!" he protested. "That means my fifty-one won't count, and I shall have to bat all over again."

"What are you moaning about?" said Venables. "Two innings on one day and you're *still* not satisfied. How about us having to field twice running! Some people want jam on it!"

At 3.15 pm the match was re-started and Jennings and Pettigrew strode to the wicket to open the innings for Drake. At 3.17 pm Jennings was back on the bank with the rest of his team and the entry in the score-book read: *Jennings bowled Venables*—0 . . . It was a tragic anticlimax to an afternoon that had started off with such high hopes.

"Really mouldy swizzle! Really unfair," Jennings grumbled as he threw down his bat in disgust. "Just wait till I see rotten old Darbishire again, that's all! Just wait till I see him."

His wish was soon granted. For as he was unbuckling his pads the errant scorer, in person, came sauntering up from the direction of the main building clutching a wet cloth in one hand.

His face was wreathed in smiles and sticky with the traces of ice-cream which he had just been consuming in the school kitchen.

Jennings glanced at the approaching figure in baffled fury. "Darbishire! Where on earth have you been?" he thundered.

The elusive scorer returned the greeting with a friendly smile. "Just now, d'you mean? I've been indoors polishing off a plate of ice-cream. Miss Matthews gave me some for helping Mrs Hackett lay the tables for tea." Unaware of his friend's feelings, he prattled on, "Really great ice-cream it was, too. I was going to try and smuggle a dollop out for you in my handkerchief only it was a bit runny, so I thought . . ."

"Don't talk to me about runny ice-cream." Jennings' face was scarlet with anger. "You're a rotten double-crossing, treacherous traitor and you deserve to be— deserve to be—" On the spur of the moment he was unable to think of any form of torture hideous enough to avenge such a dastardly crime. "Well, I never thought you'd do such a rotten trick and I've finished with you for ever."

Darbishire stared at his friend in blank amazement. "What on earth are you waffling about?"

"Don't try to make out you don't know! Sloping off

like that and stuffing yourself to the eyebrows with ice-cream when you were supposed to be scoring!"

"Oh that!" Darbishire gave a little, helpless shrug. "It was Old Wilkie's fault, honestly—it was nothing to do with me. You see, he sent me indoors to fetch a cloth and then the Head sent me to the kitchen to report to Miss Matthews and she sent me to the dining-room to help Mrs Hackett."

The explanation did nothing to soothe Jennings' feelings. "But what about the match, you addle-pated clod-poll! We've just had to start it all over again. I've had to go in twice!"

"Lucky old you!" Darbishire replied tactlessly. "Nobody picks me for even *one* innings—let alone two."

It was clear from his flippant tone that he had no idea of the disastrous consequences of his absence from the scoring-box. "How many runs did you make?"

"I made a duck as it happened," Jennings growled.

"Oh, well, not to worry! We all have an off day some times," Darbishire consoled him. "Better luck next time, eh?"

"No," said Jennings. "It was better luck the time before—when I made the only fifty I've ever scored in a House match."

Darbishire's face fell and his eyes opened wide as the full meaning of his truancy became clear.

"You made fifty!" he gasped in wonder.

"Yes, but it doesn't count, seeing you were too busy having your ice-cream nosh-up to put it down in the score-book."

"Oh, my goodness! I'm terribly sorry, Jen," Darbishire mumbled.

"So I should perishing well think. And it's not only my fifty I'm worrying about. What's everybody going to say if Drake loses the match, all because of you!"

Darbishire was so shattered that he could only stand staring, goggle-eyed with remorse, and flipping his fingers in dismay. "This is terrible," he blurted out. "Isn't there anything I could do. Couldn't I . . .?"

"No, you couldn't," came the curt reply. "You've done enough damage for one afternoon, already."

Defeated, Darbishire trudged off to the scorer's box, the damp cloth trailing from his hand. As he approached, Atkinson glanced up from the score-book and said, "You'd better keep out of Old Wilkie's gunsights till he's cooled down a bit. He looked in a moment ago and just about blew his top when he found you hadn't washed all these notices off."

"I couldn't help it, honestly. The Head sent me to . . ."

"Tell that to Old Wilkie—not me, I'm only the scorer," Atkinson returned shortly. "And I wouldn't even be the scorer if some people didn't let their House down by mooching off just when everybody was relying on them."

Darbishire relieved his feelings by attacking the writing on the wall with unnecessary vigour. It was really unfair, he told himself as *Frying Tonight* faded beneath the onslaught of the wet cloth. The whole thing was really unfair! Through no fault of his own—well, *hardly*—he had failed Drake in its hour of need. His name would be Mud for evermore! And even if it *was* his fault as everybody (including his own conscience) seemed to think, it was just an accident that might have happened to anybody. Wracked with guilt he finished his task and slunk back indoors to return the cloth, making a detour to avoid his colleagues on the playing field.

As it happened, Darbishire's lapse had no effect upon the outcome of the match; and though the game was not finished that afternoon, Drake House was already heading for victory when stumps were drawn for the day.

Chapter 5

A Bird in the Hand

By tea-time Jennings' resentment against his friend was wearing off. So much so, that after the meal was over the two boys went off to the attic together, reunited in a joint conspiracy to avoid meeting the master on duty on the back staircase.

Jennings unlocked the door and they scuttled inside. All the food had vanished from the window-sill and the bird was perched in its usual place under the eaves. Gingerly, Jennings opened the window and scattered some more corn and seed on the sill; and after a wary, sideways look the pigeon left its shelter and strutted along the ledge to inspect the offering.

The boy remained motionless as the bird came towards him and began pecking at the corn. Then, without fuss or flurry he stretched out his arm and took a firm hold of the bird's body, his thumb across the middle of its back and his fingers grasping the stomach and the folded wings.

Somewhat to his surprise the pigeon offered no resistance. Accustomed to being handled, it allowed Jennings to lift it head first in through the window as, with his free hand, he smoothed down its wings and settled its tail feathers into place.

Darbishire had been so tense with expectancy while this was happening that he had not dared to draw breath. Now that the climax was over he exhaled like an inner tube that had just passed over a tin-tack.

"Well done, Jen! What's that just above his claws? Has he got a message?" he breathed excitedly.

Jennings examined the bird's leg and shook his head.

"No, but he's got a metal ring with something stamped on it."

"Probably his name and address, so we can write and tell the owner. What does it say?"

Jennings screwed up his eyes to decipher the marking. "N 720 NU 67," he read out.

"That's hopeless. No use at all," Darbishire objected. "You couldn't just write that on a postcard and expect the postman to know where to deliver it."

"No, but it's a clue. We'll have to find out who to get in touch with, that's all," Jennings replied. He released the bird's leg and resumed stroking its wings and talking to it softly in an effort to make it feel thoroughly at ease.

For a while Darbishire stood beside him smiling indulgently at the pigeon like a fond parent at a school concert; but as the minutes passed he began to grow worried about the consequences of staying out of bounds for too long at a time.

"Come on, Jen. Old Wilkie will start panicking if he finds we're not playing about outside with the others," he prophesied. "Put old Pigeon-toes back on the sill and lets—" He broke off and frowned at the low beam traversing the attic just above his head. "I thought this was supposed to be a top security operation," he said severely.

"So it is," Jennings agreed absently, his attention still focused on the bird in his hand.

"In that case, you must be off your trolley." Darbishire pointed accusingly at the name *Jennings* pricked out in brass-headed drawing-pins running across the beam. "How about that for giving the game away. A master's only got to poke his head round the door—"

"Nobody would. The door's always locked," Jennings pointed out.

"What about old Robinson coming in to inspect the ball-cock or something! He'd be sure to report a thing like that."

Jennings pulled a face. "I hadn't thought of that," he admitted. "Better take them out right away, hadn't we!" Gently he replaced the pigeon outside on the sill. Then with his penknife he started easing the drawing-pins out of the woodwork and returning them to the cardboard box still lying in a far corner.

Darbishire watched with growing impatience. "How much longer are we going to stay up here?" he demanded anxiously. "What about Old Sir!"

"He'll probably think we're newt-spotting down by the pond,' Jennings replied. "Anyway, if you're in such a flap, don't just stand there—help me get these pins outs."

Unwillingly, Darbishire produced his penknife and set

to work, and very soon all the drawing-pins were back in the box and nothing remained of Jennings' inscription but a pattern of faintly perceptible pin-pricks on the beam.

"That's got rid of the evidence." Jennings slipped his penknife back into his pocket. "I'll just leave a handful of food for old Beak Face's breakfast, and then we'll go."

The pigeon had retreated to its roosting place under the eaves when Jennings went back to the window. So far things were going well: the bird had accepted him without protest and allowed him to handle it and examine its ring number.

They'd have to think of a proper name for it while it was in their custody, he decided. You couldn't call a top grade racing pigeon old Beak Face or Pigeon-toes. Something more respectful was needed. As he sprinkled the corn and closed the window the bird gave him a beady wink and flapped its wings: it might almost have been expressing approval of its new protector.

Jennings winked back and waved his hand. "Good night, Swing-Wing," he said. "That's what we'll call you, so mind you don't forget it!"

"Funny sort of name for a pigeon," Darbishire remarked as they left the attic. "Swing-Wing is what they call those aircraft designed by variable geometry—whatever that means."

"It's obvious what it means: it's because it varies," Jennings explained, locking the door behind him. "It's like, say, for instance in a geometry lesson when Old Wilkie says, 'Draw two identical triangles.' Well, you know how one triangle always comes out a bit different from the other, however hard you try—that's what they call variable geometry."

Darbishire pondered the explanation and shook his head. "I wouldn't like to fly in one of your planes, Jen," he decided as they pattered down the stairs. "You'd have the starboard passengers taking off while the portside passengers were doing a forced landing. Just as well *our* Swing-Wing is only a bird."

Atkinson was waiting on the playground when the two boys trotted outside in the fading evening sunshine. "How did you get on?" he wanted to know.

"Fantastic!" said Jennings. "That corn Mrs Hackett brought us is just the job. He went belting into it like a combine harvester. And the ring number on his leg is N 720 NU 67, so now we can find out where he lives."

"And take him back to his owner on our Sunday walk," Darbishire added hopefully.

Jennings turned on his friend in exasperation. "*Take* him back!" he echoed. "You must be off your runners!"

"Well, we can't look after him for ever. His owner's probably going up the wall wondering where he's got to."

"Yes, but we can't take him back, just like that," Jennings argued. "These racing pigeons—well, he *looks* like a racer—and they travel hundreds of miles. He probably lives in Barcelona or Oslo or somewhere."

Darbishire frowned and rubbed his nose thoughtfully. He had vaguely assumed that the bird must have strayed from the loft of some local fancier. If, however, they had to extend their search for an owner over the whole of Europe they might well find that the task was beyond them.

Atkinson was more optimistic. "Well, at any rate, we know his number, so all we've got to do is to look him up in the directory and then send him back," he said

Darbishire pointed accusingly at the name Jennings, "How about that for giving the game away?"

without a thought for all the difficulties involved.

"But where do we find the directory?" Darbishire objected. "You can't just pop into a telephone box and look up a pigeon as thought he was a taxi rank."

"Couldn't we ask Mr Carter, or somebody?"

"No, we flipping well couldn't. This is a secret operation," Jennings interposed firmly. "There'll be a frantic hoo-hah if we bring the masters into this."

"I don't see why. We're only trying to do the owner a good turn."

"Yes, but look at all the rules we've broken already, and we've barely started yet," Jennings retorted. "First, we've been going into a locked room that's out of bounds and letting ourselves in with a tuck-box key that nobody even knows we've got. And on top of that we got round Mrs Hackett to smuggle pigeon food in without anybody knowing, and we couldn't let her take the blame if there was a row about that."

"Well, we've got to get him back to his owner somehow," Darbishire insisted. "It'd be nearly as bad as stealing him, otherwise."

They were still discussing the problem when the dormitory bell rang, and it was not until Monday evening that they were able to meet again to discuss the best method of locating Swing-Wing's owner.

All through Mr Wilkins' maths lesson that morning Jennings had been giving the matter a great deal of thought; and when, after the bird's evening meal, the conspirators met behind the scoring-box for a full-scale discussion, he was ready to propound a foolproof solution.

"It came to me in a flash while Old Wilkie was nattering

about square roots and all that old rhubarb," he began, when Atkinson had ceased bombarding Darbishire with plantain stalks. "I suddenly remembered that it's this week Matron said I'd got to go to the dentist's for a check-up."

"I don't see how that'll help," Atkinson demurred. "The dentist won't have pigeon owners marked on his list of patients."

"No, but don't you see, this gives me a chance to spend the afternoon making inquiries in Dunhambury with no questions asked."

Darbishire looked puzzled. "How can you make inquiries if you don't ask questions?"

"I didn't mean that, you clodpoll," Jennings said impatiently. "The point is I've got a perfect excuse to be away from school from lunch-time till tea on Thursday without the masters wanting to know where I am every ten minutes."

Although the boys were not normally allowed to make the five-mile journey to the market town of Dunhambury without supervision, exception was made in cases of visits to the dental surgeon.

By skilful planning, Jennings' appointment could serve as a genuine reason for an afternoon out, for, provided that their credulity was not overstrained, masters would be willing to assume that the dentist had kept his patient waiting. And by "accidentally" missing buses on purpose, a three-fifteen appointment could be stretched to cover an indefinite period of time away from school premises.

In theory, the plan appeared to be sound. He would catch the 2.40 bus into Dunhambury, Jennings explained and, all being well, would be away from the dentist's by about half-past three. If, by good management, he contrived to miss the four-thirty bus he would not be able to catch another one until five-fifteen and would thus have an hour and three-quarters to devote to his inquiries.

"There's bound to be somebody in a town like Dunhambury who's got a racing pigeon register," he went on. "I can ask at the post office, the public library or even the police station, and as soon as I get this guy's address I can beetle off and get him to look up N 720—whatever it is—on his list and then we can send old Swing-Wing back where he belongs."

"How shall we send him?" Atkinson demanded. "By post? . . . *By pigeon post?*"

Jennings shrugged. "Perhaps by train would be easier," he decided. "With a note saying we've looked after him so well that he wouldn't leave us of his own accord."

Darbishire pondered the suggestion for a moment and said. "Well, if you're so sure you can find out where to send him, why not take him with you and drop him off at the railway station before you come back?"

There was something to be said in favour of Darbishire's amendment. Merely to return to school with the required information would entail a further journey into Dunhambury to despatch the bird to its owner. This would be difficult— perhaps impossible—to arrange if no more visits to the dentist were contemplated.

"That's a good point, Darbi," Jennings conceded. "If I do the two jobs at once it'll be killing two birds with one . . ." He broke off, frowning. In the circumstances the simile was unfortunate. "I'll borrow old Temple's fishing basket for a cage and put a note in asking the bloke to send it back."

"Better take a label, too, for when you've got the

address," Atkinson advised. "If you send him *carriage forward* you won't have anything to pay this end."

Jennings nodded, fumbling in his pocket for a pencil and a scrap of paper. "I'll plan it out properly like a military operation," he said. "If you put everything down in writing you can't go wrong."

On the back of a tattered envelope he wrote:

OPERATION SWING-WING
Thursday June 29th

14.40 hrs	Catch the twenty to three bus to Dentist with Swing-Wing.
15.15 hrs	Leave fishing basket in Waiting Room and ask Someone to mind it.
15.30 hrs	Go to Post Office etc, and make Inquiries, etc.
16.15 hrs	Get expert to look up number in pigeon directory.
16.30 hrs	Accidentally miss the half-past four bus, if asked.
16.45 hrs	Take S.W. to Rly Stn and write his label.
17.00 hrs	....

He was still jotting down details of the operation when the dormitory bell summoned the conspirators to bed.

Chapter 6

Operation Swing-Wing

Temple was more than willing to lend his fishing basket
when he was informed that the success of the project
depended upon his co-operation.

"Yes, of course you can borrow it, but I shall want it
back afterwards," he told Jennings and Darbishire in the
dormitory on Monday evening. "So mind you put a note
in telling this guy in Stockholm or wherever it's going, to
post it back when he's finished with it."

"Not to worry! Jen's going to get the letter written
tomorrow so it's all ready for Thursday," Darbishire
assured him as they stood at the wash-basins together,
foaming at the mouth with pink toothpaste. "We're bound
to get a letter back thanking us, and perhaps even a
certificate of merit from the International Racing Pigeon
Lost Property Office, or whatever it's called."

The composition of the letter to be enclosed in the

fishing basket caused Jennings a great deal of thought when he settled down to the task during break the next morning.

"The trouble is I don't know who I'm writing to until I've had the ring number looked up by this bloke in Dunhambury," he complained to Atkinson who had offered to help with the letter. "It'll be all right if the man lives in England, but if we've got to send old Swing-Wing halfway across Europe how do I know he'll understand English?"

"We could get Henri to make a copy in French and put that in too," his colleague suggested.

"M'yes!" Jennings was still not convinced. "But supposing the guy's a Dane or a Dutchman or even a . . ."

"Oh, for goodness' sake!" Atkinson protested. "You'll never get the letter written in *any* language if you're going to argue till the bell goes. The guy will just have to use his loaf that's all."

After a few false starts which finished up in the waste-paper basket, Jennings produced a letter which he decided would meet all requirements. It read:

> Linbury Court School,
> Sussex,
> England.

Dear Sir, Herr, Monsieur or Signior (as the case may be),

I hope it is all right to write to you in English, as I am a British subject, but if you only speak Norwegian or something, I hope it is all right. The enclosed racing pigeon, Number N720NU67 in your language, but we call him Swing-Wing in English, has been roosting on the window-sill outside the attic for about three weeks or more and will not fly away, so I will get your address from a man in Dunhambury whom I do not know yet and despatch goods *per* rail. Please send the fishing basket back because Temple wants it.

    Must stop now as I am running out of ink.

            Yours sincerely,

                (Singed) J. C. T. Jennings.

Henri Dufour had a great deal of difficulty making a copy in French as he could not really understand what it meant in English. However, he did his best!

Wednesday was an anxious time for the pigeon-fanciers, for their plan depended upon Swing-Wing's co-operation. For four days now, Jennings had succeeded in coaxing the bird along the window-sill for its food and taking it in his hand when it approached. Even so, the bird was wary and any incautious movement was enough to send it fluttering away to the roof.

On Monday evening, for example, Darbishire had sneezed at a critical moment and it had taken twenty minutes of coaxing and wheedling to persuade it to return. Any delay of this sort would completely upset the conspirators' timetable if it happened on Thursday.

"The bus won't wait while you hang out of the attic window crooning like a foghorn," Atkinson pointed out to Jennings after school on Wednesday. "The only thing to do is to get him in the basket first thing after breakfast tomorrow morning, so he'll be ready."

As it happened, this part of the plan worked more

smoothly than they had expected. Mr Hind was on duty on Thursday, and while Jennings hurried upstairs to the attic immediately after breakfast, Darbishire detained the duty master in the hall with a long and rambling story about a missing pair of house shoes.

A few minutes before the bell rang for morning assembly Jennings appeared at the stairhead smiling and clutching his left ear as a signal to Darbishire that his mission was accomplished, and that it was now safe to allow Mr Hind to proceed on his tour of duty.

At two o'clock Jennings cleaned his teeth and collected his bus fare from Matron's dispensary. A quarter of an hour later, when afternoon school began, he avoided the boys streaming into the classrooms and slipped away to the attic. When he came down again carrying the fluttering fish-basket, the corridors were empty and his route to the school gates was clear.

The bus arrived on time and the twenty-minute journey to Dunhambury passed without incident. Swing-Wing was docile and appeared quite at home in his container: and this was natural enough, Jennings decided, for as an experienced racing pigeon the bird must have spent many hours in a basket travelling to the starting point of his races.

Jennings was allowed to leave Swing-Wing with the receptionist while he went into the dentist's surgery. The inspection was soon over, and shortly before half-past three he strode into the post office in Dunhambury High Street and approached the counter at a position marked *Licences*.

"Good afternoon," he said to the young woman who

looked up to serve him. "Can you possibly tell me the regulations about racing pigeons, please?"

"You don't need a licence for pigeons," she replied. "Only for guns, motor vehicles and television sets—that sort of thing."

"No, I don't mean that. I just wanted a copy of the instructions about where to find out about the numbers on their legs."

She looked puzzled, so Jennings explained his problem, but she was still unable to help. Turning, she called to the assistants farther along the counter: "Anybody know anything about racing pigeons?"

Nobody did, and Jennings was about to leave when a uniformed postman who was filling a sack with parcels paused in his work and said. "Hey, wait a minute though! What about old Stan Goodman at East Brinkington. He keeps homing birds—at least, he used to."

The postman dumped his sack by the back wall of the office and came forward to the counter. "You go and see old Stan, son. He'll put you right, if anyone can. Lives in that cottage just opposite the church. Anyone will tell you. Kept pigeons for years, he did."

Stan Goodman. East Brinkington. Opposite the church. Jennings wrote the information down on a licence form, thanked everybody profusely and took his leave. It was not until he was outside on the pavement that it occurred to him that he had no idea where East Brinkington was. He was about to go back and ask his friendly postman for directions when a green single-decker bus trundled up the High Street and drew to a halt at the Post Office stop.

Jennings glanced at the front of the vehicle and noticed

57

the name of East Brinkington amongst the villages at which the bus was due to call. Without further inquiry he jumped aboard and sat down on the seat nearest the platform with the precious basket on his knee.

It was not until the bus had started that he began to wonder whether he had been rather rash. East Brinkington might be a suburb just outside the town, or it might be a village ten miles or more away. Could he spare the time? Could he afford the fare? Should he abandon his journey and jump off at the next stop?

He was debating the matter when the conductor approached and was able to set his mind at rest.

"East Brinkington? About three miles. Be there in less than ten minutes," he informed his passenger.

Reassured, Jennings bought a ticket and then sat looking out of the window. As soon as they were clear of the town the bus left the main road and followed a winding route through the surrounding country. The road was narrow and though they met little traffic the bus had to pull right in to the side every time a car or a tractor approached from the opposite direction.

Jennings had no idea where he was. This was new territory to one who seldom went farther than Linbury village during term time. This was an adventure—a secret journey into unknown surroundings in quest of vital information. He felt so excited that he laughed out loud: this was a better way to spend an afternoon than merely popping into the dentist's for a routine check-up!

"What's the joke, mate?" the conductor asked. It was rare in his experience for solitary passengers to find the scenery amusing.

"Oh, nothing really. It's just that..." Suddenly, Jennings wanted to talk—wanted the man to know just how exciting the project was. "Well, it's a secret really, but I don't mind your knowing if you promise not to spread it." He glanced over his shoulder to make sure that no other passengers were listening. "It's all to do with a scheme called Operation Swing-Wing."

"Operation *what*?"

"Swing-Wing—you know, variable geometry and all that. And I've got to go to East Brinkington to find a man who may have certain vital information: and all the time Matron thinks I'm still having my teeth inspected in Dunhambury."

This made no sense to the conductor. Was the lad trying to be funny, he wondered? Or should he have had his brains inspected as well as his teeth? Playing for safety, he nodded at the fishing basket and said, "Brought yourself a picnic tea, eh?"

"No, this isn't a picnic. This is a pigeon."

"Uh?"

"Yes, a homing pigeon—a racer. He's the one I've got to go and see this man at East Brinkington about," Jennings went on as though the explanation should now be clear. "Only, you see, I don't know my way around these parts and I haven't got much time so it wouldn't do to get lost, would it?"

A slow grin spread over the conductor's face. "You'll be all right, mate," he said. "If you get lost you can always ask the pigeon. *He'll* know his way home."

The village of East Brinkington nestles in a fold of the

South Downs. It boasts the finest scenery and the worst bus service for many miles around.

So much seemed obvious to Jennings as, five minutes later, he stood by the bus stop in the village street watching his single-decker bus disappear round the bend of the road. The bus company's time-table was affixed to the bus stop, and from this he had just learned that there was no bus back to Dunhambury until after 6 pm.

This was disastrous! This made nonsense of Operation Swing-Wing! Come what may, he *must* be back in Dunhambury in time to catch the 5.15 bus back to school, having first despatched the pigeon to its owner from the railway station.

This was no time to panic, he told himself severely. Surely he could get a lift back into the town somehow. Perhaps this Mr Goodman would run him there by car. In any case the time was only ten minutes to four. He still had nearly an hour and a half to complete his mission— and a great deal could happen in an hour and a half.

Glancing along the village street, Jennings noticed the spire of the parish church a hundred yards away. This was the landmark he was looking for, so he made his way past a row of cottages until, approaching the churchyard gate, he came to a footpath running back from the road. A few yards along the footpath was a whitewashed cottage with a small garden where a middle-aged woman was unpegging a row of washing from a clothes line.

Mrs Goodman, no doubt! Jennings let himself in through the garden gate and trotted up the path, the fishing basket bumping up and down against his thigh at every step.

"Good afternoon," he called out as he hurried forward. "Excuse me, but I was told to come here by a postman in Dunhambury because your husband is an expert on pigeons... That is, *if* I've come to the right place and you're Mrs Stan Goodman," he added as an afterthought.

"That's me all right," she replied through a mouthful of clothes pegs. "But if it's my husband you want, you'll have to come back this evening."

"This evening!" he echoed. "Can't I see him now?"

"Stan's never at home in the daytime," she told him. "He won't be back from work till six o'clock."

She sensed his disappointment and asked what the trouble was; and as she seemed a friendly sort of person and a sympathetic listener he told her the story of Swing-Wing and how important it was for him to consult an experienced fancier.

"And I can't possibly wait till Mr Goodman comes home because I wouldn't get back till ever so late, and I obviously wouldn't be at the dentist's all that time, would I?" he finished up.

Mrs Goodman suggested the obvious answer. "Why not leave the bird here in our loft, then?" she said, indicating a small outbuilding at the bottom of the garden. "My husband can easily send it back to its owner when he's found out who it belongs to."

Jennings beamed her a smile of pure gratitude. "Hey, that's really great of you. Are you sure you don't mind?" He was delighted at this neat solution to his problem and thankful, too, to be relieved of his responsibilities before the situation had got beyond his control. "OK, here he is then," he said, slipping the strap from his shoulder and laying the basket on the ground.

Kneeling, he fumbled with the fastening and threw back the lid.

"He's ever so tame, honestly," he went on as proudly as though he had trained the bird himself. "He lets you pick him up and . . ."

He broke off in astonishment as, without warning, Swing-Wing shot out of the basket and flew straight up into the air.

Jennings made a grab at the bird, but it was useless. To his dismay it soared over his head, high above the garden and then set off in an easterly direction flying fast and gaining height all the time.

Very soon there was nothing to be seen of Swing-Wing but a high-flying speck in the afternoon sunshine.

Chapter 7

Emergency Call

Mrs Goodman picked up her washing-basket.

"That's that, then!" she said with a shrug. "It was asking for trouble, taking the lid off like that. They always fly straight up, those racers. Trained to it, you see."

There was nothing Jennings could say in defence. "I know. I mucked it up properly that time," he admitted.

"I wouldn't say that. Best way, really, seeing as he'll be safely home in a few hours time, as like as not," she replied. "It'll save Stan having to write and find out who it belongs to."

The bird was out of sight, but Jennings still stood staring in the direction it had taken. The sun was behind him so Swing-Wing was flying east. How far had he to go, the boy wondered? ... Amsterdam? ... Oslo? ... Helsinki? ... Or perhaps only to Eastbourne. It was a fascinating question and now, it seemed, he would never know the answer.

"You think he'll get back all right?" he asked anxiously.

"He knows his way," she told him. "You mark my words, you've seen the last of that pigeon."

Jennings picked up the fishing basket and slung it over his shoulder. Even though Swing-Wing's unexpected escape had made things easier for all concerned he could not help feeling annoyed at the bird's sudden departure. All the trouble that he and Darbishire and Atkinson had taken for its welfare! All those furtive visits to the attic, dodging Mr Wilkins on the back stairs! All the hair-raising hazards of Operation Swing-Wing! If it was determined to fly home of its own accord, why couldn't the wretched bird have gone yesterday, or last week or—well, some time before he—J. C. T. Jennings—found himself faced with transport problems to which there seemed no answer.

"It's all very well for *him* belting off home like that," he said bitterly. "How does he think *I'm* going to get home before the Head starts sending out search parties and things?"

Mrs Goodman was sympathetic, but having no means of transport at her disposal, could only offer advice. She thought for a moment and said, "Your best plan would be to take the short cut through Boland's Wood to Hickley's farm and then past Three-Acre Marsh to Birchingdean. You can pick up a bus into town from there at twenty to five, if you look sharp."

The place names meant nothing to Jennings. "Is it far?" he asked. "Would that be quicker than walking back to Dunhambury the way my bus came?"

"Much quicker; it's a short cut," she assured him. "There's extra buses from Birchingdean that don't come round these parts. I often go to Dunhambury that way, shopping."

It seemed the only sensible thing to do if it meant that he could get back to school on time.

"Righto, then! Which way do I go?" he asked.

Mrs Goodman described the route in such detail that Jennings was unable to keep all the directions in his head. The important thing, it seemed, was that once he had passed Hickley's farm he must follow the lane and on no account veer off on any of its numerous by-paths.

"Trust me! I'll find it all right," he assured her as she escorted him to the garden gate. "And thanks ever so much for—well, for what you *would* have done if old Swing-Wing hadn't flown off in a panic like that."

The footpath twisted its way uphill from Mrs Goodman's cottage to the outskirts of Boland's Wood. Here it continued on the far side of a stile, and ran for some distance through a spindly copse and past clumps of bracken as far as Hinkley's farm.

So far the route was easy to follow, but when he had left the farmyard behind him Jennings began to wish he had paid more heed to his guide's directions. "Follow the path," she had said. But the farther he went the more difficult it became to decide which of the criss-crossing intersections was the main path and which were the by-ways.

He began to grow worried. One false turn and every step would be taking him farther and farther away from the bus he was hoping to catch at—at? He wracked his brains trying to recall the name of the village Mrs Goodman had mentioned. It began with a B—he knew that.

Burlington? Buckingham? Brinkington? It couldn't be the last because he had just come from there.

At that moment the path branched into two separate tracks leading off in opposite directions. Jennings stopped dead, staring first along one and then along the other. There was nothing to indicate which of the two he should follow.

He knew then that he was lost. Hopelessly lost in a lonely tract of country, and he couldn't even remember the name of the place he was trying to find. And more-over—he glanced at his watch—if he didn't find it soon it would be too late, because the bus was due to leave in just over ten minutes.

A wave of self-pity splashed over him. They'd all be playing cricket back at school, or perhaps just coming in with Mr Wilkins to get ready for swimming: Darbishire, Venables, Temple—all of them playing about, laughing their heads off without a care in the world. In Jennings' mental picture of the scene even Mr Wilkins seemed to be smiling!

With an effort he pulled himself together, and ran off down the right-hand track as fast as he could. After a few hundred yards the footpath emerged on a country road, but there was no signpost and once again Jennings came to a stop wondering which way to turn. As he did so, he noticed a thatched cottage along the road to the left.

Perhaps there was someone there who could help him on his way! He started towards it and then stopped dead in surprise ... From an outhouse in the garden, thick white smoke was belching from a window and billowing towards the thatched roof of the cottage in menacing curls.

Jennings forgot his own troubles in the face of this emergency. Racing through the garden gate to raise the alarm, he almost collided with an elderly woman, white-face with anxiety, who came hobbling down the path with the aid of a stick.

"Quick! Quick! The barn's alight!" she cried distract-edly. "All that straw—it'll set the house on fire if we don't stop it."

Jennings glanced past her and saw that the flames were licking the lintel of the outhouse door. Instinctively he started to run towards it, but the old woman called him back.

"It's no good. You can't get in," she gasped. "Go and get the fire brigade before it spreads to the thatch. We're not on the phone here."

"Is there anyone here to help you?" Jennings asked breathlessly.

She shook her head. "They're out on the tractor down Four Acre way. Can you ride a bike?"

"Yes, of course."

She indicated an enormous, old-fashioned machine propped against the cottage wall. "Take that, then—and hurry."

"Yes, but I don't know where . . ."

"The phone box is down that way," she pointed along the road. "Second left, first right and then left again. Tell them to come quick."

Jennings raced for the bicycle and scooted with it down the garden path and turned left into the road. It was the heaviest and clumsiest bicycle that he had ever ridden and it was with difficulty that he managed to swing his leg over the saddle. Once mounted, he found he could only reach the pedals at the top of their stroke, and could do no more than jab at each one as it circled past its highest point.

This was useless! So he slipped forward off the saddle on to the cross-bar and in this way was able to propel the creaking machine along at a fair pace.

His own problems forgotten, he pedalled along without a thought of what would happen when eventually he got back to school. At the moment the burning barn was the only thing in his mind. There was no one else to summon help: everything depended upon him.

He had no idea how far he would have to go to find the telephone kiosk. "Second left, first right, then left again," the old lady had said. Or had she? Now he couldn't be sure. For the second time in fifteen minutes he faced the dilemma of a doubtful decision. And this time a mistake would mean disaster!

The road twisted and forked for half a mile and Jennings was beginning to think he must have taken a wrong turning when, reaching the brow of a hill, he saw a telephone box by some crossroads at the bottom of the downward slope.

Stamping hard on the pedals, the cyclist sent his machine hurtling down the hill at full speed. As he approached the crossroads he tugged on the brakes... Nothing happened! The old bicycle sped onwards, gaining speed all the time.

Desperate now, Jennings turned the wheel to the left and the machine swerved up the nearside bank into a

Jennings and the old bicycle parted company at the bottom of the hill.

hedge, shooting the rider over the handlebars to land on a grass verge running alongside the road.

Fortunately, the landing was soft and Jennings wasted no time wondering whether or not he was hurt. He scrambled to his feet and, leaving the machine up-ended in the hedge, rushed into the telephone kiosk and snatched the receiver from its rest.

He dialled 999, and almost immediately heard the operator asking him which emergency service he required.

"Fire brigade, please," he answered breathlessly. "It's urgent. There's a sort of barn full of straw burning away like anything and it'll set light to the thatch on the cottage if they don't come quickly."

The voice at the other end of the line sounded calm and business-like. "What is the address of these premises?"

The question hit him like a blow on the ear. His eyes opened wide and his jaw dropped.

"The address?" he echoed blankly. "Oh, my goodness. I'm terribly sorry, *I don't know*!"

"You don't know!"

"Well, no, not really. You see I—" It sounded ridiculous, but he would have to admit it. "Well, I can't tell you the address of this place because I forgot to ask."

Never before had Jennings felt so helpless and so humiliated. He must have been mad, he told himself, to rush off like that without stopping to think. But it was too late now for self-reproach. The operator was saying: "Just keep calm and take your time. If you saw this fire yourself, you must have known where you saw it. Right?"

Jennings gulped hard. She was trying to help him and it wasn't any use. Couldn't she see that it was ignorance and not panic that was the cause of his trouble!

"I know where the fire is, but I don't know the address of the place," he insisted. "I'm a stranger round these parts, that's why."

"Where are you speaking from?" the operator asked.

This was easy. The telephone number was staring him in the face. "Birchingdean 4283. It's a call box, you see."

She repeated the number and said. "A fire appliance will be leaving immediately. Please stay by the telephone kiosk until it arrives."

Chapter 8

News Item

Jennings replaced the receiver and went outside, where he stood leaning against the glass panels of the kiosk mopping his brow and recovering his breath.

He hadn't given a very good account of himself on the telephone, he thought. The operator had spoken to him as though he was too flustered or too half-witted to make himself understood. He wanted to ring her back and assure her that he was as cool, calm and collected as anyone could be who had just taken a header over the handlebars.

He walked back across the road and inspected the up-ended bicycle. The front wheel was buckled and the spokes were splayed out at all angles. He hoped no one would hold him to blame for that: it was just another incident in the chapter of accidents that had befallen him ever since the afternoon's plans had started to go wrong.

How long would the fire engine take, he wondered? Not knowing where he was, he couldn't tell how far it would have to come. All he knew was that there was now no chance of his getting to Dunhambury in time to catch the bus back to school. He'd be in real trouble this time he told himself, if he failed to arrive on the 5.15. Matron would telephone the dentist, the headmaster would telephone the police and it would be impossible to keep his escapade a secret. There would be a most frightful row and . . .

His train of thought stopped with a jolt as, literally, a most frightful row assailed his ears. It was the wail of the fire-engine's siren as the appliance sped along the narrow road towards the phone box.

Jennings wasn't expecting it so soon. They'd been quick, wherever they'd come from, he thought, glancing at his watch.

The time was ten minutes to five—just an hour since he had got off the bus at East Brinkington with Swing-Wing. He could hardly believe that so much had happened in so short a time.

The siren ceased as the appliance, a water-tender, rounded the bend and pulled up at the crossroads. As Jennings ran towards it the sub-officer opened the door and called out, "Was it you who made the fire-call, son?"

"That's right," Jennings confirmed. "It's a cottage somewhere around these parts. I can't tell you how to get there because of all the turnings, but I could show you, if you'll take me with you."

The officer hesitated. It was strictly against regulations to carry members of the public on an appliance when proceeding to a fire. On the other hand it was clear that they would not be able to locate the outbreak until too late unless they had someone to guide them. He'd have to take a chance: there was no other way.

"Hop in quick, then," he said, stretching out an arm and hauling the boy up into the cab beside him. At the same moment the vehicle shot forward as Jennings pointed up the hill to direct them on their way.

It was only a short distance back to the cottage, but for Jennings it was the proudest journey of his life. Sitting squashed on the front seat, giving instructions about the route gave him the thrill of seeming to be in charge of the operation.

"Turn right here ... Left at the next one, just past that tree," he called out as the appliance streaked along the winding road with siren sounding and blue light flashing.

This was the life, he thought! If only Darbishire could see him now! But there was little enough time to bask in glory, for in a mere three-quarters of a mile the trip was over. As the appliance screeched to a halt outside the gate and the crew leaped down, Jennings noticed that the straw-filled barn was still burning fiercely but, so far, the cottage was untouched.

Three or four farm-workers had arrived while Jennings had been away, but lacking any proper equipment there was little they could do to help. Now, they hurried forward to lend a hand while the old lady stood back casting anxious glances at the thatch on her cottage roof.

In a matter of moments the firemen had a jet of water on the flames to prevent the fire from spreading, and another playing on the cottage roof to cool down the thatch.

It took a little time to reduce the flames to smoke, but as soon as they were able to get close enough the firemen forced their way inside the burning barn. The straw was ruined and they made no attempt to salvage it: instead, they dragged the scorched and smouldering bales away from the heart of the fire into the open and allowed them to burn out under control.

As Jennings stood by the gate watching, the old lady came down the garden towards him.

"I want to thank you for calling the brigade," she said. "I don't know what I should have done if I'd been all by myself."

"Oh, that's all right. It was just lucky I happened to be around," he replied. A thought struck him and he added, "Er . . . about your bicycle: I'm awfully sorry but it hadn't got any brakes and I had to do a sort of crash-landing in the hedge and . . ."

"Don't worry about the old bike. It was due for the scrap-heap long since," she assured him. "So long as it got you to the phone box that's all that mattered!"

She hobbled off to speak to one of the firemen and almost immediately three vehicles arrived in quick succession. First came a staff car from Dunhambury Fire Station, then a police car and finally a small white saloon driven by a bearded young man in a light tweed suit.

Vaguely, Jennings wondered who this newcomer might be: he seemed on familiar terms with the police and the fire officers, for he spent some moments chatting to them before picking his way over the hose and across the cluttered garden to where the old lady was standing.

He was probably the insurance man assessing the extent of the damage, Jennings decided; for he had produced a notebook and was asking her questions and jotting down the answers. She must have made some reference to the part that Jennings had played in summoning help, for soon afterwards the man strolled back to the gate where Jennings was standing and said. "Hallo, young man! My name's Gray. I've been hearing things about you. I gather it was owing to you that the brigade arrived so quickly."

"Well, yes. The lady asked me to telephone," Jennings agreed. "The operator thought I needed my head examined, but it was only because nobody told me the address of this place."

Mr Gray seemed interested. He asked Jennings his name, his age, where he lived and where he went to school and recorded all the information in his notebook.

"How are you getting back to Linbury?" the young man asked when the interrogation was over.

"That's just the trouble. I don't know. I was hoping to catch the five-fifteen from Dunhambury, but it's too late for that now," Jennings told him. "There'll be a frantic hoo-hah if I'm not back by quarter to six because everybody thinks I've gone to the dentist."

Mr Gray looked faintly puzzled. "What—with a fishing basket?"

"Oh, that!" Jennings had forgotten he was still bearing Swing-Wing's container slung around his neck. "That's nothing to do with the dentist—well, it *was* to begin with, but that's all over now."

The young man did not pursue the subject. Instead, he said, "Well, if you're stuck for a lift, I'll run you back to Linbury. We'll just about beat the bus if we go now."

Jennings' eyes opened wide in grateful surprise. "Hey, would you really! That's really great of you."

"Why not! There's nothing more to see here, now they've more or less got the fire under control. Hop in my car and we'll get going."

Jennings was about to obey when he remembered the rule. "Oh, but I'm afraid I can't," he demurred. "We're not allowed to accept lifts from people we don't know."

Standing close at hand was the uniformed driver of the police car who had happened to overhear the conversation. He gave Jennings a friendly tap on the shoulder and said, "You'll be all right with Mr Gray, lad. We all know him around these parts. He's almost part of the scenery."

The young man grinned. "That's right! Well known to the police. How's that for a reputation!"

Jennings considered. If the police were willing to vouch for Mr Gray, there could surely be no harm in accepting a much-needed lift. "OK, then. Thanks very much," he said as he got into the car. This was a stroke of luck that he had not been expecting. If the kind young man succeeded in getting him back to school in time there was a good chance that the facts about Operation Swing-Wing would never reach the headmaster's ears, after all.

It was about seven miles back to Linbury—a mere

fifteen minutes' journey in Mr Gray's car. On the way they chatted about cars and cricket and swimming, and though the young man did most of the talking it wasn't until they stopped outside the school gates that he happened to mention the reason why he had been present at the scene of the fire.

"Here we are, then. We've beaten the bus by at least two minutes," Mr Gray remarked as Jennings got out of the car. "So you're back on schedule with nothing to worry about."

"Thanks to you," Jennings said gratefully. "It's been the most exciting afternoon I can remember, what with the fire and everything. The only thing is," he went on in a voice tinged with regret, "the only trouble is my friend Darbishire and the others will never believe me when I tell them I actually rode on the fire engine and told them where to go."

Mr Gray laughed. "They'll believe it all right next Thursday," he said. "Just show them the *Dunhambury and District Gazette*. It'll have all the details—if my editor's in a good mood."

Jennings stared at him in sudden comprehension.

"You mean you're a reporter?"

"That's right. All the local news—fires, baby-shows, council meetings—the lot. Just leave it to Johnny Gray."

The sudden revelation hit Jennings like a douche of cold water. The local newspaper was delivered to the school every week: the headmaster read it, Mr Wilkins read it—*all* the masters read it! What, then, was the point of trying to keep his escapade a secret if the news was to be blazoned forth in black headlines all over the

Dunhambury and District Gazette? The prospect was horrifying! . . . Disastrous!

"Yes, but look here, just a minute," Jennings began.

But it was too late. Mr Gray's foot was on the accelerator and it is doubtful whether he even heard the boy's protest. With a friendly wave he let in the clutch and the car shot off in the direction of Dunhambury.

Jennings stared after it in helpless indecision. He was still staring when, two minutes later, the five-fifteen bus from Dunhambury pulled up near the school gates, giving him his cue to return to a life regulated by school bells and governed by school rules.

The excitements of the afternoon drained away through the soles of his shoes, and he trudged up the drive in a mood of black despair.

Even so, his misfortunes were not ended. Darbishire and Atkinson were waiting for him on the playground and came running towards the dejected figure with the fishing basket as soon as he appeared round the bend of the drive.

"What happened? What went wrong?" Atkinson greeted him. "I thought you were going to send Swing-Wing back by train, *carriage forward*. You didn't half bish up the issue!"

Jennings stared at his friends in puzzled wonder. Even though that part of the operation had not gone according to plan, it was impossible that Atkinson and Darbishire, safely at home on the cricket field, could have known of his failure.

"Why? What do you mean?" he asked.

By way of reply Darbishire pointed towards the window-sill of the tank attic where a racing pigeon could be discerned preening its feathers in the early evening sunshine.

"He came back," Darbishire said simply. "Suddenly zoomed down over the cricket pitch at about quarter-past four. Trust you to go and make a right royal carve-up of the job!"

Jennings said nothing. He'd had a very worrying afternoon and his feelings were too deep for words.

Chapter 9

The Worm in the Wood

It had come as a great shock to Darbishire and Atkinson, during cricket practice, to see Swing-Wing fly in from the west, soar across the cricket field and come to rest on the attic window-sill.

Darbishire, fielding at mid on, was so astounded that he stood gaping up into the sky just as the easiest catch in the history of cricket came spooning up from Blotwell's bat towards him—and landed on the turf at his feet!

The fielding side seethed with exasperation.

"*Darbishire!*" they groaned in derision, holding their heads and marking time with their feet. "You great, butter-fingered, mole-eyed, hibernating tortoise! You did it on purpose! You didn't even try."

Mr Wilkins, umpiring at the bowler's end, added his reprimand. "For goodness' sake wake up, boy! You deserve to be punished for wilful inattention . . . Inexcusable wool-gathering!"

"Sorry, sir," the wool-gatherer apologised. "I didn't see the ball coming."

"You *should* have seen it. It's your business to watch the game."

"Yes, I know, sir, only I just happened to look up and . . ." He paused, remembering the security precautions. "I—er—I unexpectedly saw a bird, sir."

"Saw a bird! What sort of an excuse is that!" Mr Wilkins demanded. "You don't imagine that a Test Match at Lord's comes to a complete standstill every time some wretched sparrow flies over the ground, do you!"

Binns, the youngest boy in the school, who was fielding close at hand was impressed by Mr Wilkins' fanciful illustration. "Sir's quite right, Darbishire," he shrilled at the top of his penetrating voice. "Supposing you were playing for England in about ten years' time and suddenly an albatross or a golden eagle escaped from the Zoo and came swooping down and perched right on your nose, you wouldn't be able to . . ."

"That's enough, Binns," the umpire said curtly. "Nobody's likely to pick Darbishire to play for England in a *hundred* years—let alone ten."

"Ah, no sir, because he'd be over the age limit in a hundred years, but, say, for instance . . ."

"Quiet!" boomed Mr Wilkins. "Get on with the game." And turning again towards the pitch he roared, "Play!" in a voice that startled Swing-Wing on his window-sill, sixty feet up and a hundred yards away.

Thus it was that Darbishire, in particular, was agog to know what had gone wrong with the plans as he and Atkinson accompanied Jennings indoors on his return.

"I'm too hungry to talk about it now. You'll have to wait till I've had something to eat," Jennings told them when they plied him with questions.

School tea was over, but owing to Jennings' "official" leave of absence at the dentist's, his meal had been put aside and was awaiting him in the dining-hall. Strictly speaking, Darbishire and Atkinson had no business to go with him, for, except at meal times, the dining-hall was not a room which the boys were entitled to use: but as Mr Hind, the duty master, was known to be bowling at the cricket nets there was little risk of discovery. So they all went in together, and between mouthfuls of tinned salmon and beetroot salad, Jennings recounted the events of the afternoon.

At first they didn't believe him. There was no doubt about Swing-Wing's escape, of course, for they themselves had witnessed his return. But the ride on the fire appliance strained their credulity to breaking-point. . . . That was the sort of thing that only happened to other people. Such fantastic good fortune was beyond the wildest hopes of those whose dreary day-to-day existence was bounded by boarding-school life and irksome school rules.

"It's true, anyway—every word of it," Jennings assured them when the tale was unfolded: and his tone was so earnest that eventually they had to believe him. "I only wish it wasn't."

"You only wish *what*!" Atkinson stared at him in flabbergasted amazement. "You must be off your trolley! You land yourself feet first in the most supersonic adventure since the Battle of Hastings and then you calmly turn round and say you wish you hadn't!"

"Oh, I enjoyed it all right—it was terrific," Jennings agreed. "And I was dead chuffed about getting back without being caught, too. But that's not going to help me next Thursday when that wretched local paper comes out!"

He certainly had a point there! They fell silent, brooding over what seemed to be an insoluble problem. Finally, Darbishire said, "Couldn't you write to this reporter guy and ask him not to put it in?"

Jennings shook his head. "You can't muzzle the press like that. And anyway, even if Mr Gray *did* agree, I bet his editor wouldn't—and he's the boss."

"That's right," Atkinson confirmed. "You know what these local papers are like. Half the time they've got nothing to put in except old Women's Institutes and somebody riding a motor-bike without a rear light. So now they've got a really exciting fire to write about they're bound to give it the full treatment, whatever you say."

Darbishire nodded in agreement. In his mind's eye he could already see the front page account. Aloud he quoted: "*The fire brigade was summoned by J. C. T. Jennings, aged eleven, in brackets, of Linbury Court School . . .*"

"*While supposed to be on a visit to the dentist's,*" Atkinson added with relish. "That'll put the Head into orbit when he reads it. I wouldn't like to be near the launching pad when the Archbeako's rocket takes off."

"Oh, shut up," Jennings said irritably. "It's all old Swing-Wing's fault, really. I wish now we'd never tried to help him. I wish we'd left him to look after himself."

"It's too late to talk like that now," Darbishire pointed

out. "He's relying on us to feed him. Why else d'you think he came back!"

"Well *you* can flipping well feed him for a bit, then, I've had enough." Jennings pushed back his chair and rose from the table. "I've got more urgent things to think about between now and next Thursday than changing his water and doling out handfuls of pigeon mixture."

As the boys emerged into the hall, Mr Carter was coming down the stairs. He glanced at Jennings and said, "So you're back at last! The dentist certainly kept you a long time. I was beginning to think something must have gone wrong."

Jennings forced a wan smile and mumbled, "Oh, no, everything was quite all right, sir."

And indeed, it *was* all right at the moment, he consoled himself, as the master passed on down the corridor. But what was the use of that when the storm was certain to break with next Thursday's issue of the *Dunhambury and District Gazette*!

Darbishire and Atkinson gave Swing-Wing his meal that evening. It was only fair, Darbishire confided to Atkinson as he replenished the pigeon's drinking water from the cold tank in the corner of the attic—it was only right and proper to give poor old Jennings a short break from his duties as chief pigeon-fancier when he had so many problems on his mind.

"It wasn't like him to say he wished we'd never started looking after Swing-Wing," Darbishire observed with a frown. "It's all this chasing about on fire engines and hobnobbing with the press. I expect he'll be feeling better tomorrow when he comes down to earth again."

But on the morrow a new development occurred which, in a somewhat roundabout way, was destined to have a bearing upon the events of the following week.

During the morning when all the boys were in school, Matron was busy in her dispensary on the second floor. Suddenly, the sound of water splashing down from a height caught her ear and she looked out of the window seeking the cause. Away to her left where the building made a right-angled turn, an overflow pipe jutted out from under the eaves, and from here a stream of water was cascading down in a sixty-foot waterfall.

Robinson, the school caretaker, was mopping the floor outside the dispensary as Matron hurried out on to the landing.

"Slight flood!" she announced. "I don't know what's causing it, but there's a miniature Niagara Falls spouting out from somewhere under the roof."

Robinson followed her back into the dispensary and glanced out of the window.

"It's that ball-cock on the cold tank got stuck again," he diagnosed. "Nothing to worry about, Matron. I'll just get my keys and nip up and fix it."

"Keys?" She sounded mildly surprised. "Why do you bother to keep a room locked that's got nothing in it except a cold water tank?"

"Because of the boys, Matron—that's why," he replied in resigned tones. "If I didn't keep it locked they'd be breeding tadpoles or something in that tank, as like as not."

"Oh, surely not! They all know perfectly well that the attics are out of bounds."

He gave her a wan smile and trudged off in search of his keys, shaking his head over the credulity of sympathetic school matrons. Out of bounds it may have been, but in Robinson's long experience as a school caretaker, only a lock and key was proof against small boys intent on getting up to mischief.

He climbed the back stairs, let himself into the attic and made for the cold water tank in the far corner. As he expected, he found that the ball-cock had stuck and was submerged beneath the surface, so that the water continued to flow in through the inlet pipe and escape to waste through the overflow.

It took only a few minutes to put the matter right. Then, satisfied that all was well, he strode back towards the door—and bumped his head sharply on the beam traversing the room.

"Cor!" Robinson rubbed his injured forehead and glanced at the offending woodwork. They'd no right to stick beams where people could walk into them, he thought. He might have knocked himself out!

He was about to proceed on his way when he noticed that the spot where he had hit his head was marked by dozens of tiny holes extending along the beam in an irregular pattern.

He narrowed his eyes and examined the marks as well as he could in the light filtering in through the small window. Knowing nothing of Jennings' experiment with the drawing pins it was understandable that Robinson should jump to a false conclusion. After all, the tiny holes *looked* like woodworm.

Nasty stuff, woodworm, Robinson reflected as he trudged out of the attic and locked the door. Last term it had been Dry Rot in the tuck-box room and before that Death Watch Beetle in the linen cupboard. And now the worm! Tut! If they went on like this they'd be getting Bats in the Belfry next. Muttering to himself he went downstairs to break the news of the latest bacteriological invasion.

During staff supper that evening Matron passed on the information to the headmaster.

"Robinson tells me that the beam in the attic has got the worm," she remarked as she served the soup. "Absolutely riddled with it, he says."

"Really!" the headmaster pursed his lips and raised his eyebrows. "That could be serious; it's extremely difficult stuff to get rid of, if it's not caught in time."

"It's natural enough in old timber," Mr Wilkins observed from across the table. "I've got a little gadget like a spray-gun that I bought to treat that antique bookcase in my study. It did the trick, too: there isn't a trace of worm left since I went over it, injecting a squirt in all the little holes."

Mr Pemberton-Oakes shook his head. "It sounds as though the damage will require rather more drastic treatment than you could undertake with your—ah—little gadget, Wilkins," he said. "If what Robinson says is correct we may well find that the whole of the top floor—indeed all the timber in the roof—is already infested."

Anxious to be helpful, Mr Wilkins persisted. "It may

not be so bad as you think, HM. In any case, it wouldn't do any harm if I took my little gadget up there and had a look."

"Do, by all means, if you want to," the headmaster replied, spreading his table-napkin on his knees. "But to be on the safe side I think I'll get in touch with one of these firms that specialise in timber preservation. I'll get them to send a man along to make a thorough inspection."

Chapter 10

The Two-Pronged Plan

In spite of what he had said about the impossibility of muzzling the press, Jennings decided, early the following week, to try to get in touch with Mr Gray.

"There's just a chance," he informed his colleagues in Dormitory Four at bedtime on Tuesday. "I know it's a pretty feeble one—but if I could get him to look at it from my point of view, I'm sure he'd be willing to hush it up."

Darbishire sat up in bed. "Why not? He's only got to leave your name out. He hasn't got to write the account all over again," he argued. 'Tell him to say: *The fire was reported by an unknown passer-by who happened to be— er—passing by when it caught fire.*"

"Or he could say: *The brigade was summoned by a mysterious stranger who vanished into thin air after his errand of mercy was performed*," suggested Venables.

Although not on the roster of official pigeon-fanciers, both Venables and Temple had taken a lively interest in Swing-Wing ever since his adoption as a secret pet. From his bed by the window Temple said, "Well, you'd better get a move on, Jen. It's Wednesday tomorrow and the paper will be lying on the doormat by breakfast on Thursday. I should ring him up, if I were you."

The advice, though well meant, was not easy to put into practice. Boys were not allowed to use the telephone without permission, and anyone attempting to put a call through from the extension in the hall would be in full view of any member of the staff who happened to come down the stairs at an inconvenient moment.

"You'd have to choose your time, of course," Temple went on. "Like, say, for instance, in about half an hour from now while all the masters will be having supper."

"That'd be crazy," Jennings objected. "Mr Gray wouldn't be at the office at this time of night. You seem to forget it's only a tiddly little local newspaper doing flower shows and things. It's not the sort with ace-reporters dashing about in helicopters, telephoning from Tokyo at three o'clock in the morning."

Temple shrugged. "OK, have it your own way, but if you don't have a bash now while the going's good, you'll be properly up the spout."

"I'll do it tomorrow," said Jennings, putting off the evil moment. "There's bound to be a chance when there's no one about."

As it happened, the chance came in the middle of the afternoon when the school were out on the playing field watching a first XI match.

Jennings sat on the bank between Darbishire and Henri Dufour. Mr Carter was umpiring and Mr Wilkins, Mr Hind and all the other masters were watching the game from benches beside the pavilion—all except Mr Pemberton-Oakes who had been seen to go out in his car shortly after lunch. Matron was busy upstairs in her dispensary: Jennings could just see the top of her head from where he sat. Every member of the staff was accounted for. This was surely the time to act!

He nudged Darbishire and spoke in a low tone. "I'm going indoors to ring up the *Dunhambury Gazette*. Shan't be long."

Darbishire gasped at the boldness of the plan. "What, now? In broad daylight! Supposing somebody comes beetling along!"

"There's nobody left to beetle." Jennings indicated the row of reclining masters, and the nurse's cap bobbing about at the dispensary window. "It'd need a bomb to shift Old Wilkie and Co this side of the tea interval. If I go now, I'll be laughing."

So saying, he edged his way backwards up the slope and crawled twenty yards on hands and knees behind the screen of boys lining the bank. Then, safely out of the masters' vision, he jumped to his feet and scuttled into the building at full speed.

It was cool indoors after the warm sunshine outside—cool and strangely quiet, without the customary clamour of seventy-nine pairs of juvenile footwear drumming along the corridors.

The telephone was on the hall table with the directory lying beside it. Jennings flicked through the pages and found that the *Gazette* had three different telephone numbers. He chose one at random and dialled.

For a long time the bell went on ringing and nobody answered the call. What sort of a newspaper office was this, Jennings thought bitterly! Why, for all they knew, they might be missing the most sensational news-story of the year!

Then, just as he was about to replace the receiver and try one of the other numbers, the ringing tone ceased and an elderly female voice sounded in his ear. "Hallo," it said, without enthusiasm.

"Oh, hallo! Is that the *Dunhambury and District Gazette*? I want to speak to Mr Gray, please."

"Mr Gray? He's not here."

"Well, may I speak to the editor then?"

"He's not here, either. Nobody's here. Nobody at all."

"*Nobody!*" Was he speaking to a ghost, Jennings wondered!'

"Only me, that is," the ghost explained. "This is the canteen, see. They're all upstairs in the top office, looking through tomorrow's paper."

"Tomorrow's paper!" Jennings felt weak at the knees. "You mean it's been printed already?"

"Well, of course. Goes to press Wednesday mornings," she said. "If you want the editor, you'd better ring . . ."

"It's all right, thanks. It doesn't matter," Jennings broke in. He knew now all he needed to know. "It was about tomorrow's paper, you see, only it's no good speaking to Mr Gray if there's no chance of . . ."

Suddenly, footsteps sounded behind him. Wheeling round, Jennings saw the headmaster approaching from the direction of the front door. His unexpected return was something that the boy had not reckoned on. It was too late to move away from the telephone, for Mr Pemberton-Oakes had already seen him, so with great presence of mind he continued talking. "No, this isn't Linbury General Stores—this is Linbury Court School," he said, and firmly replaced the receiver.

"Wrong number, eh?" the headmaster observed pleasantly as he strode into the hall. "You do know, of course, Jennings, that boys are not normally allowed to answer the telephone when it rings?"

"Yes, sir."

"However, I agree that one cannot allow the telephone to go on ringing indefinitely when no member of the staff is at hand to cope with the call," the headmaster went on. "So I suppose it would hardly be fair, on this occasion, to take you to task for a breach of school rules."

"Yes, sir. No sir. Thank you, sir," Jennings mumbled as Mr Pemberton-Oakes, smiling indulgently, proceeded up the stairs.

Jennings' forehead was furrowed with thought as he made his way back to the cricket field and took his place on the bank beside Darbishire.

"Well, did you get through to Mr Gray in his office?" his friend asked eagerly.

"No, I got through to someone called 'Only me' in the canteen," Jennings replied. "I've had my chips this time, Darbi. She told me it had been printed already."

Darbishire winced in sympathy. "Wow! Headlines and all? *Linbury Court Boy Hero of Famous Fire*—and all that?"

"How do I know what the headlines are?" Jennings returned irritably. "I never asked her. She probably wouldn't have known anyway, down in the canteen."

"Yes, but surely . . ."

"There's only one thing to be done," Jennings went on, frowning and staring at the cricket field but seeing nothing. "I'll have to think of a plan to confiscate the paper before it gets to the staff-room."

"Oh, no! Not *another* plan!" Darbishire groaned in dismay. "Your ribby old plans always come unstuck at the joints." By way of proof he pointed towards the attic window-sill where Swing-Wing, sunning himself in his favourite spot, appeared to be watching the cricket match with mild interest. "Look at that! According to your rotten old plans he ought to have been back in Moscow or somewhere a week ago: instead of which we still have to go foxing up the back stairs with fistfuls of dried peas when there's nobody about."

Jennings looked aggrieved. "It was Swing-Wing who mucked up the last plan—not me," he pointed out. "And anyway, seeing the trouble I'm in, I should have thought the least you could do was to . . ."

"All right, all right!" Darbishire put in hastily. He knew from experience that it was useless to argue with Jennings when his mind was made up. "What's the great idea going to be this time, then?"

"Give me a chance! How do you expect me to think with you nattering down my ear all the time! Get on explaining the rules of cricket to Henri, while I make my plan of campaign."

By the time the juniors left the cricket field for the

swimming pool Jennings had decided what to do: and after tea that evening he summoned Darbishire and Atkinson to a secret meeting behind the shoe-lockers.

"I've worked out what you might call a two-pronged plan of attack and it'll need the three of us to make it work," he told his not-too-willing confederates. "An advance guard down at the school gates, and a second line of defence in the hall in case he gets through."

"In case *who* gets through?" Atkinson demanded.

"The guy who brings the papers—that red-haired bloke on a green bike with a bag on the back."

A working knowledge of the things that always happened in the half-hour before breakfast had stood Jennings in good stead when making his plans. He knew from observation that the red-haired cyclist from Linbury General Stores and Post Office arrived on his paper-round within a few minutes of seven-forty-five every morning. He knew also that half-a-dozen or more weekly and daily papers would be squeezed singly through the letter box to land on the doormat, where they would be retrieved by Robinson (who was usually mopping the hall floor at that time) or by one of the masters on his way to breakfast. It would be difficult—but not impossible—to intercept the papers at this stage and remove the *Dunhambury and District Gazette* from the pile. Far easier would be to meet the paper-roundsman at the school gates and offer to save him the trouble of cycling up the drive.

"That's where you come in, Darbi," Jennings went on, as he outlined his plan. "At half-past seven you nip out of the side door into the bushes and fox down to the gates without anyone seeing you. Keep under cover until you hear his tyres scrunching on the gravel, and then pop out and stop him. He'll probably be really pleased to let you take the papers up to school for him."

Darbishire had little enthusiasm for the role chosen for him. "And what do I do with them?" he demanded suspiciously.

"You stick the *Dunhambury Gazette* up your sweater and fox back through the bushes and hide it in your tuck-box," Jennings explained. "Then you go round to the front door and bung the other papers through the letter-box just as the delivery bloke would do."

"Supposing he won't stop! Supposing he won't give them to me! It's all very well for you to dream up plans for other people to carry out, while you just sit back and . . ."

"I shan't be sitting back. Atki and I have got the trickiest part to cope with, if anything goes wrong down at the gate."

In this, the planner was right. The second line of defence might, indeed, be a complicated manœuvre requiring not only a cool head but some skill in sleight of hand.

It was well known that Mr Wilkins, of all the masters, was the most eager to inspect the morning papers and would often be waiting in the hall for their arrival.

If, therefore, the paper-boy managed to elude the guard at the gate, Jennings and Atkinson would be on hand to put the alternative plan into operation. It would be Atkinson's duty, the leader explained, to engage Mr Wilkins, or any other passing adult, in light conversation and divert his attention away from the front door at the first rattle of the letter-box.

Meanwhile, Jennings would station himself on the doormat. He would gather up the papers as they fell, surreptitiously pushing or kicking the incriminating journal under the doormat, to be retrieved later when the coast was clear.

"I'll hand them over to Old Wilkie or whoever it is," he told them. "He probably won't notice the *Gazette* is missing, and even if he does he'll just think it's missed the early delivery and may be coming later."

The assistant-conspirators exchanged doubtful glances.

"What d'you mean—keep them talking and looking the other way?" Atkinson demurred. "I may not be able to think of anything to say."

"Use your gumption. If it's Mr Carter, offer to show him your stamp album, and if it's Old Wilkie say something like—well, does he think the West Indies is better than Australia."

'How d'you mean, *better*? Better for what?"

"Cricket, of course, you clodpoll—what else?"

"Well I *hope* it works all right," Darbishire said gloomily. "Only if I suddenly come belting out of the bushes waving my arms like a hitch-hiker the bloke might have a heart attack and fall of his bike."

"So much the better," Jennings said unfeelingly. "He won't feel so much like cycling up the drive if he's just come a cropper over the handle-bars."

Chapter 11

Front Page Splash

Mr Wilkins was the master on duty on Thursday. As he was shaving, soon after the rising bell, he remembered that it was his sister's birthday at the weekend. Unfortunately, he had done nothing about buying her a present, so the least he could do at short notice would be to send her a greetings card to mark the day. Mr Wilkins frowned in thought. From breakfast time onwards he would be far too busy supervising the boys to go down to the village shop. On the other hand he would have plenty of time if he went straight away: there was sure to be someone to serve him, for the stationery counter opened early to cope with the delivery of the morning papers.

As soon as he was dressed he hurried downstairs and out through the front door on his early morning shopping expedition. It was not worth the trouble of getting his car out of the garage for so short a journey, so he grabbed his bicycle from the rack and set off down the drive at a lively pace.

Five minutes later the side door opened and a slim figure crept furtively out and scampered into the cover of the laurel bushes. So far as Darbishire was aware the duty master was still in his bedroom, but he was taking no chances of being spotted from an upstairs window. He crouched in the shelter of the bushes for some moments while he peered round to make sure that no one was about. Then he made his way through the thick shrubbery running alongside the drive until he was within a few yards of the school gates.

Here he stopped and hid in the foliage of a syringa tree, satisfied that he was concealed from all angles. Unfortunately, his vision was limited and he could not see the gates away to his left. But this was not important, Darbishire assured himself, for he was only a few feet from the drive and the scrunch of tyres on the loose gravel would warn him of the delivery boy's approach.

So far, so good! The nervous feeling of butterflies fluttering in his stomach now gave place to a tingling excitement. He, C. E. J. Darbishire, had been chosen as the Spearhead of the Attack. He felt proud and important. Come what may, he would not betray his leader's trust.

He glanced at his watch: it was twenty minutes to eight. If the paper-boy arrived on time he would be back indoors a quarter of an hour before the breakfast bell, with the vital evidence tucked up his sweater. He would have time to . . .

Darbishire gave a nervous start as the scrunching sound he was waiting for assailed his ear. Stooping, he peered through the branches and caught sight of a bicycle wheel ten yards away.

Now was the time! Breaking cover he dashed out on to the drive waving his arms and calling, "Hey there! Stop! Whoa! Stop!"

Then he skidded to a halt and his jaw dropped and his eyes opened wide in horrified dismay.

For the cyclist was not the red-haired roundsman on the green bicycle: it was L. P. Wilkins Esq, MA, pedalling briskly through the gate with a tasteful birthday card in his pocket.

Mr Wilkins was so startled by the apparition of the frantic signaller bursting out of the bushes that he wobbled unsteadily and nearly fell off his machine. Then he recovered, pulled on his brakes and put his foot to the ground.

"What in the name of thunder are you playing at, Darbishire?" he demanded in perplexity. "What were you doing in those bushes?"

"Er—just coming out, sir."

"I can see that, you silly little boy. That doesn't explain why you came bolting out like a rat from a drainpipe, shrieking your head off and wailing like a banshee as soon as I turned the corner. What are you up to?"

Darbishire shifted from foot to foot in embarrassment. Caught off his guard, he couldn't for the life of him think of a reason for his eccentric behaviour. "I—I don't know, sir," he stammered.

"You don't know! You *must* know!"

Darbishire wracked his brains, but the search produced nothing plausible. "I heard a bicycle coming," was hardly a convincing explanation, but it was all he could think of.

"Well, go on, boy!" It was clear that Mr Wilkins was not going to let his victim off the hook. "Civilised people don't jump out of bushes endangering the life and limb of passing cyclists just for the fun of it."

The culprit stared down at the gravel and mumbled: "I—er—I thought you were the paper-boy from Linbury Stores, sir."

"Why? Do I *look* like the paper-boy?"

"No, not really, sir. Only I was going to offer to carry the papers up to school to—er—to save him the trouble."

"Very generous of you, but I'm quite sure the paper-boy is capable of doing his round without your help," Mr Wilkins said with a grunt of disapproval.

By now he had formed his own opinion to account for Darbishire's presence in the shrubbery at so early an hour in the morning. It was a wrong deduction, as it happened, although it seemed to fit the facts, and the boy's grubby knees and soil-stained hands seemed to strengthen the impression still further.

"Well, I'm warning you, Darbishire—and you can pass it on to all your bug-hunting friends with my compliments," the master continued. "If there's any more nonsense of this sort, in and out of the bushes, I shall ask the headmaster to put a stop to this business of collecting caterpillars and things before breakfast."

Collecting caterpillars! Why, of course! At least a dozen of the younger boys set forth on some sort of insect-hunt every morning. Here was the perfect excuse to have explained his presence in the shrubbery and he'd never even thought of it! However, as Mr Wilkins had jumped to this conclusion, there was no point in shattering his illusions.

"Off you go indoors, Darbishire," Mr Wilkins went on. "Go and wash your hands. You're not going into breakfast with half the topsoil of the shrubbery plastered all over your fingers."

He stood watching as the Spearhead of the Attack, his mission a failure, turned and trotted obediently up the drive towards the school buildings.

Jennings and Atkinson were already manning their posts in the second line of defence when Darbishire came into the hall to tell them what had happened.

"Tut! Trust you to go and make a carve-up of it," Atkinson said scathingly when he heard the news.

"I couldn't help it," Darbishire defended himself. "How was I to know . . .?"

He broke off as Robinson came into the hall carrying a mop and a bucket of soapy water.

"We'll switch over to the other plan," Jennings commanded in a whisper. "The papers should be here in a minute, so if Old Sir's still outside putting his bike away there's just a slight chance . . ."

But the slight chance died on his lips as, hard on the heels of Robinson, Mr Carter and Mr Wilkins strolled into the hall together chatting about England's chances in a forthcoming Test Match.

The conspirators exchanged helpless glances. How could they hope to succeed with the odds so heavily against them!

"Have the papers come yet?" Mr Wilkins said breezily,

... the three conspirators saw the first newspaper drop straight into the bucket of soapy water ...

as Robinson set down his bucket and started his daily chore of mopping the floor.

"Not yet, sir. Be here any minute now," the caretaker informed him.

"Good! There should be an article in the cricket column about . . ."

"Sir, please sir, would you like to come and see my stamp collection," Atkinson broke in, remembering his instructions.

"Not before breakfast, I wouldn't," the master returned shortly. His glance travelled round the hall noting the anxious expressions of the conspirators as they tried to appear relaxed and at ease. "What's the matter with you boys? What are you hanging about in the hall for? What's going on?"

His questions were met by puzzled frowns and looks of wide-eyed innocence. "Hanging about, sir? *Us*?" the puzzled frowns seemed to be saying. And the innocent looks, deeply offended, appeared to be murmuring, "Whatever makes you think that? *We've* got nothing to hide."

"It's quite obvious there's *something* going on," Mr Wilkins persisted, turning to his colleague. "First of all, Darbishire comes cavorting out of the undergrowth doing a tribal war dance and accusing me of being an employee of Linbury General Stores. Now, we find the three of them lurking about like cats round a bird-bath waiting for something to happen."

Mr Carter smiled and said nothing. He knew from experience that if Mr Wilkins *really* wanted to know what was afoot, he was going the wrong way about it.

The patch of damp floor spread as Robinson worked his way round the hall. By now he had reached the area by the front door, where he stooped down and dragged the doormat out of his way.

The boys looked on in despair. Robinson had removed the vital camouflage and had set down his bucket on the very spot where the incriminating evidence was to have been concealed.

This was a catastrophe! This was the final blow: and all the time Mr Wilkins was standing there watching them, awaiting some sort of explanation for their continued loitering. When none was forthcoming he said, "Well, I don't know what you boys think you're playing at, but whatever it is, you're not going to do it here. Off you go, the three of you, and wait in the common-room till the bell goes for breakfast."

"Yes, sir."

The unhappy procession lined up and straggled off across the hall in single file. But they had not gone five paces when the sound of heavy boots ascending the front steps came wafting through the panels of the door. The letter-box rattled as the flap was pushed open and a folded newspaper appeared in the aperture.

The procession stopped and wheeled round, unable to wrench their gaze away from the scene of the disaster . . . And as they watched they saw the first of the papers drop straight into the bucket of steaming, soapy water standing on the spot normally covered by the front doormat.

Robinson saw it too, and jumped forward—too late to avert the accident, but just in time to pull the bucket away as the second newspaper came tumbling through the flap.

"Tut—tut—tut! Cor! Look at that," the caretaker grumbled, scowling at the sodden journal immersed in its bath of detergent. "I put my bucket there for two shakes of a lamb's tail, and now look what's happened!"

The rest of the papers came slithering through the slot to land safe and dry at Robinson's feet. Shaking his head over the mishap he picked them up and handed them to Mr Carter.

"What shall I do with this other one?" he asked, nodding towards the bucket. "P'raps I could dry it out a bit if anyone wants to read it." By way of experiment he put his hand in the bucket and tried to lift the paper clear of the water. It came up in a steaming, soggy pulp which disintegrated in his hand and slid down on to the floor in a shapeless mass.

"That's that, then," Mr Carter observed. "You'd be wasting your time trying to salvage that nasty-looking mess. You'd better put it in the dustbin."

"Which paper was it?" Mr Wilkins demanded. "I hope it wasn't the *Guardian*. I particularly wanted to see the cricket page."

Which paper was it? His query was echoed in the minds of the three conspirators still standing on the far side of the hall, forgotten in the flurry and fuss of the last sixty seconds.

Robinson screwed up his eyes trying to decipher the sodden inscription. "It's all right, Mr Wilkins; it's not one of the dailies," he said at length. "It's the *Dunhambury and District Gazette*."

"That's all right, then." Mr Wilkins was not at all worried by this deprivation. "There's never anything worth reading in the local paper, anyway." He glanced round and saw Jennings, Darbishire and Atkinson almost dancing with pent-up emotion which they dared not express out loud.

The duty master glowered suspiciously. A couple of minutes ago they had been wrapped in a pall of gloom: now they were trying to stifle grins of joy and delight.

"Have you gone off your heads, all of a sudden?" he demanded. "What are you so excited about?"

Jennings pulled himself together and avoided Mr Wilkins' eye. "Nothing really, sir. Well, nothing worth talking about. We just thought it was rather funny when the paper did a nose-dive into the bucket, sir."

"Did you, indeed!"

"Oh, yes, sir! Ever so funny, really!" Jennings' tone was confident now that the danger was passed, for it was unlikely that any of the masters would bother to seek out another copy of the current issue. Indeed, why should they, when they were unaware that the paper might contain anything more sensational than the usual news of local Women's Institutes and the fatstock prices at Dunhambury cattle market?

The breakfast bell rang and the boys hurried off to join their colleagues lining up outside the dining-hall. Behind them trudged Robinson heading for the dustbins with the pulpy remains of the *Dunhambury and District Gazette*.

Jennings glanced back and saw him. Good old Robbo, he thought! They would never have managed it without his help!

Chapter 12

Punishment Deferred

It was on the following morning that Mr Wilkins remembered his intention to inspect the worm-eaten beam in the attic.

Until then, he had forgotten the suggestion he had casually thrown out during staff supper the previous week, but while looking through his study cupboard for a textbook during morning break he came across the container half full of the chemical insecticide which had proved so effective in ridding his bookcase of woodworm.

The headmaster hadn't seemed very impressed with his idea of treating the beam with his little spray-gun, Mr Wilkins recalled. In fact, he had been rather scathing about the very suggestion that the operation could be tackled by an amateur. Maybe he was right; maybe the job would call for professional equipment and expert handling. But how satisfying it would be to prove that the headmaster was wrong!

The first lesson after break was a free period for Mr Wilkins. So when the bell rang he borrowed the key and took his spray-gun up to the top floor to see what he could do. He found the beam pin-pricked with dozens of tiny holes as Robinson had described, though in the dim light of the attic they were only just visible against the rough, unpainted surface of the wood.

Mr Wilkins' spray-gun was designed to deal only with limited areas of infested woodwork, for the method consisted of inserting a tiny nozzle into each hole separately and injecting a squirt of liquid by pressing a metal plunger. To do this on a large scale would be tedious, but as only a few square feet of the beam appeared to be in need of treatment Mr Wilkins decided to set about the work without delay. Choosing a hole at random he jammed in the nozzle and pressed home the plunger: then on to the next hole and the next, working his way down and along the irregular pattern of pin-pricks.

The liquid in the container was the colour of creosote, and as the wood was somewhat porous the jabs of the nozzle made dark circles around the circumference of the holes like ink dots drawn on blotting paper. With the holes set close together, the dark stain spread from one to another joining up the dots in a sequence of straight lines and curves which showed up clearly against the light-coloured background.

Mr Wilkins' suspicions were first aroused when, after a few minutes' work, he noticed that he had made a well-formed letter N. It was odd, he thought, that woodworm should eat their way into the timber in such a symmetrical pattern. He moved on to the next batch of holes, and found the damp black marks made by his nozzle running together to form another letter *N*. After that, he traced out a letter *I* and followed it with another *N* and then a *G*.

By now Mr Wilkins' suspicions had become a certainty, but he worked on, determined to reveal the telltale evidence in its entirety. When he had finished he stepped back and surveyed the result like an artist inspecting his canvas. His nozzle had pricked out the word *Jennings* in little black dots.

So much for the woodworm!

"Doh! The silly little boy!" Mr Wilkins snorted in indignation and scowled at a pigeon which appeared to be criticising his work from the sill beyond the closed window. He turned away, still scowling: it never entered his mind that there could be any connection between the feathered onlooker and the inscription on the beam. What *did* enter his mind was the fact that a boy in Form Three had been breaking bounds and deserved to be punished for the offence.

The bell rang for change of lessons as Mr Wilkins came downstairs. He went to his room to replace his spray-gun and collect a pile of exercise books, and then made his way towards Five B classroom where he was due to take a mathematics lesson. On the way he met Mr Pemberton-Oakes coming out of the staff-room.

"I've got some news for you, HM," Mr Wilkins said. "That woodworm Robinson reported in the attic wasn't woodworm at all—it was Jennings."

The headmaster's eyebrows rose in surprise. Even allowing for the fact that the school caretaker was short-sighted, he should surely be able to tell the difference between a timber-boring grub and a boy of eleven.

"Robinson thought the woodworm was Jennings?" he queried.

"No, no! The other way about. Robinson thought Jennings was the woodworm. He wrote his name on the beam, you see."

"Who did—Robinson?"

"No—Jennings did. I went along the beam with my little spray-gun just now, and when I got to the end I'd written Jennings' name."

The headmaster was out of his depth. "But you just said that Jennings had written his own name on the beam. Now you say that *you* wrote it. Really, Wilkins, I can't make head or tail of this story."

Marvelling that headmasters could be so obtuse, Mr Wilkins tried again. "I've just been treating the beam with my little gadget," he explained. "The holes weren't made by woodworm as Robinson supposed: they were made by Jennings dotting out his name with a compass point or something."

"Indeed!" Mr Pemberton-Oakes nodded in comprehension. "That means, Wilkins, that the boy has been out of bounds and will have to be punished for it."

"Yes, of course, but it means more than that," Mr Wilkins said with a satisfied smile. "It means we haven't got any woodworm, so you needn't bother to call in the experts you were talking about at supper last week." He paused, awaiting the headmaster's congratulations upon his foresight in unmasking the truth, but Mr Pemberton-Oakes merely pursed his lips and shook his head.

"It's a bit late to tell me that now, Wilkins," he said.

"I telephoned them some days ago and they're sending one of their inspectors over this afternoon."

He passed on down the corridor, frowning in thought—and had to side-step hurriedly as Binns and Blotwell, late for their lesson, came skidding round the bend with arms flailing like skaters on an ice-rink getting up speed.

"Binns! . . . Blotwell!"

The skaters slid to a stop against a radiator, performed a figure-of-eight turn and stood looking up at the tall figure of the headmaster with foreboding.

"Sir?"

But, for once, Mr Pemberton-Oakes had something on his mind, other than dealing out retribution to unofficial skating champions.

"Tell Jennings to report to me in my study immediately after lunch," he said.

Jennings couldn't think what the headmaster could possibly want to see him about when the message was relayed to him at the end of morning school. It couldn't be anything to do with Swing-Wing, he reasoned, for they had taken every care to avoid meeting masters on their journeys up the back stairs. Surely it wasn't the fire in the barn! Had the headmaster seen the incriminating evidence in some other copy of the local paper?

"What sort of mood was he in, when he told you?" he asked the messengers. "Was he looking like an ordinary sort of human person, or was he hopping mad?"

Blotwell considered. "You can't really tell with the Archbeako. He usually looks as though he's just bitten a hot potato, even when he's pleased," he decided.

"He wasn't actually frothing at the mouth, or anything, and I don't think his eyes were actually blazing," Binns added by way of consolation. "But that's nothing to go by. He's probably timing the count-down so he goes into orbit the very moment you knock on the study door."

This was cold comfort and Jennings had little appetite for the midday meal. He tried not to worry but, as his conscience was by no means clear, he could not afford to relax in case some crime of long-standing had come to light.

Darbishire brought his mind to bear on the problem as he tucked into his prunes and custard, but he, too, was unable to put forward any plausible theory. "Perhaps he wants you for something terrific," he hazarded. "Perhaps he's going to make you a prefect or congratulate you on doing well in class."

Venables, seated opposite, was so overcome with mirth at the suggestion that he choked over a glass of water and was sent out of the room by Mr Wilkins for misbehaviour.

As soon as the meal was over, Jennings went off to the study and knocked at the door. The headmaster was not in the best of moods, the boy decided, as he stood facing him across the leather-topped desk. Whatever the reason for the summons, congratulations on his progress in class seemed unlikely to be the main topic of conversation.

Mr Pemberton-Oakes looked up from a sheaf of papers and said, "I assume, Jennings, that you are aware that the attics are out of bounds to all boys."

The attics! So Swing-Wing was the cause of the trouble! But how could any of the masters have known about the bird, considering how careful they had been in covering their tracks?

"I am therefore at a loss to understand," the head-master went on without waiting for a reply, "why at some period of the term, you appear to have gone into the attics without permission and inscribed your name on the beam."

He would have to confess, Jennings decided: after all, if the Head already knew so much there was no point in trying to keep Swing-Wing's presence a secret any longer. With luck he wouldn't have to go into too much detail.

"Did you write your name on the beam?" the head-master persisted.

"Yes, sir."

"Why?"

"I saw a pigeon on the window-sill, sir."

Mr Pemberton-Oakes seemed to find the explanation puzzling. "You saw a pigeon on the window-sill!" he echoed. "I fail to see why that should fill you with an urge to scratch your name on the roof timbers with—with a compass point or whatever it was."

"A box of drawing-pins, sir."

"Very well, then, a box of drawing-pins." The head-master seemed determined to discover the link between these unconnected facts. He glanced out of the window and went on, "From where I am sitting, Jennings, I can see a starling perching on the telephone wire. Do you think that is an adequate reason for me to rush outside on to the playground and print out my name with drawing-pins on the telephone pole?"

"No, sir—not really. Not unless you felt you simply *had* to, sir."

It was clear from his expression that Mr Pemberton-Oakes did not suffer from compulsive urges of this sort, so Jennings hurried on, "It was a racing pigeon, you see, and he made a home for himself on the window-sill so we—er—I mean, so *I* went in to feed him, sir."

"I see!" the headmaster dragged his gaze away from the wire-perching starling. "You admit then, Jennings, to two offences. First, breaking bounds in the attic, and secondly, to defacing school property. The second offence, though trivial in the amount of damage inflicted, is more serious than you might suppose."

Jennings stared at a spot on the wallpaper just above the headmaster's left ear, and said nothing. He couldn't think how making a few pin-pricks on a rough old beam could be regarded as a serious offence by any stretch of the imagination.

"It so happens that your—ah—depredations with the drawing-pins were misunderstood," Mr Pemberton-Oakes continued. "As a result, various people have been put to a great deal of inconvenience and expense, for which I must hold you responsible. I shall, therefore, punish you for this—ah—nonsensical escapade: I shall punish you severely, as you deserve."

At that moment there was a knock on the door and Ivy, one of the domestic staff, came into the room.

"Excuse me, sir, there's a gentleman in the hall," she informed the headmaster. "A Mr Marriott. Come about the woodworm, he says."

Mr Pemberton-Oakes sighed and shook his head. "A

wasted journey, I fear," he remarked to the silver inkstand on his desk. "Tell him—er, no, perhaps I had better see him myself and explain that his services will not, after all, be needed." He tut-tutted in embarrassment at the thought of having to admit that he had summoned an expert on timber preservation to undertake a long journey in order to inspect the word *Jennings* in drawing-pin holes.

"Show Mr Marriott in," he said to the maid: and turning to the cause of all the trouble he barked out, "As for you, Jennings, you will report to me for punishment later, when I have dealt with the unfortunate situation for which you are entirely to blame." He indicated the door with a menacing twitch of his eyebrow. "Out, boy, out! Come back and see me after prep this evening."

Chapter 13

Reprieve!

With the prospect of a second visit to the headmaster's study hanging over him, it was no wonder that Jennings spent an anxious and unhappy afternoon.

There were still a few minutes of free time left before afternoon school when he reached the common-room, and here he found Darbishire awaiting his arrival.

"What did he want you for? How did you get on?" his friend demanded.

Jennings shrugged. "He'd found out I'd been in the attic and I've got to report back for punishment later."

"Bad luck," Darbishire sympathised. A thought struck him and he added, "What about Atki and me? Doesn't he know we've been there, too?"

"Why should he? You two had more sense than to plaster your name up in drawing-pins, and that's what gave the game away." Jennings pulled a long face. "I'm worried about poor old Swing-Wing, though. He'll have had his chips if we can't go up there any more to feed him."

The afternoon post had arrived and Mr Carter had given Venables the job of handing out the letters.

"One for you, Jen," he said, sorting through the little pile of mail he was carrying. "Business letter, by the looks of it."

Jennings took the typewritten envelope and looked at it in puzzled surprise. Nobody ever typed letters to him: his family and friends always used ballpoint pens. His wonder grew as he noticed the postmark.

"It's from Dunhambury," he announced in mystified tones. "I don't know anybody there. Well, not the sort of people who'd write me letters. Who on earth is it from?"

Venables looked blank. "I'm only the postman. I haven't got second sight," he said. "If you *really* want to know, it might not be a bad idea to open it and find out. Less strain on the eyesight than trying to read it through the envelope."

The letter bore the heading *Dunhambury and District Gazette*. It read:

Dear Jennings, (I can't call you by your first name because you only gave me your initials!).

This is just a note of apology as I know how keen you were to show your friends your name in this week's issue. So you are probably calling me all sorts of things now you have found there's no mention of it.

Blame the editor, mate—don't blame me! There

was such a glut of local news last week that your little fire item got crowded out. If your friends still think you are pulling their legs just show them this!

Sorry and all that,

Yours,

Johnny Gray.

Jennings read it through twice with Darbishire peering at the page over his shoulder. When he had finished, he stuffed the letter into his pocket and said, "Coo! Rotten old chizz! Rotten old mouldy chizz."

Darbishire looked surprised. "But you didn't *want* it to be in the paper," he pointed out. "You fell over backwards trying to get in touch with him to ask him to leave it out. You ought to be pleased."

"Pleased!" Jennings snorted in disgust. "What about all the trouble I went to trying to confiscate it with Old Wilkie and Mr Carter and Robbo prowling round the hall like vultures waiting to pounce."

"Yes, that was a bit dodgy," his friend agreed. "Especially with Sir going into orbit because I thought he was the paper-boy. My nerves haven't sprung back into shape yet." He paused and added, "Still the plan wasn't really a washout because the paper *didn't* get through to the staff-room, did it!"

"So what! It wouldn't have mattered if it *had*, now we know there was nothing about me in it. All that trouble for nothing! Tut! It's enough to give the cat the measles." Still snorting, Jennings wandered off to fetch his books as the bell rang for afternoon school.

Darbishire turned to Venables with a sigh of patient despair. "You can't please old Jen. He wants it both ways.

Still you have to make allowances. He's got a lot on his mind, just at the moment."

The load on his mind certainly played havoc with Jennings' work during school, and several times he was reprimanded by Mr Carter for inattention. He felt no better during cricket later in the afternoon and played well below his usual form. Indeed, the crowning humiliation came when Henri Dufour, desperately keen to show his prowess as a cricketer, was put on to bowl and sent down a ball which Jennings scooped up straight into the hands of cover point.

Jennings walked back to join his team-mates in a pall of gloom. He had lost his wicket to a novice (and a Frenchman at that!) who less than three months ago hadn't known one end of a cricket bat from the other. This was the final degradation. Nobody could sink lower than that!

He felt miserable during swimming, had no appetite for tea and his spirits were at their lowest ebb when the time came for him to report back to the study to hear his sentence delivered and his punishment imposed.

He knocked at the door, was bidden to enter...and found himself being welcomed by an amiable Mr Pemberton-Oakes smiling indulgently across his leather-topped desk.

"Ah, Jennings! Come in, come in!" the headmaster greeted him in tones so warm and so human that the boy stopped short in speechless astonishment. Was this some sort of brainwashing torture, he wondered? Was it some form of trick to lull his suspicions and catch him off his guard?

But it was no trick. Since Jennings' departure, Mr

Pemberton-Oakes had spent a profitable hour in the company of Mr George Marriott, area inspector of the London and Provincial Timber Preservation Co Ltd.

To begin with, the headmaster had been profuse in his apologies for bringing Mr Marriott all the way to Linbury on a fool's errand. There was no infestation of the timbers, he had assured him: the whole thing was due to a misunderstanding over a boyish prank.

"A mere piece of tomfoolery by one of the boys which I shall deal with in an appropriate manner," he had explained. "Unfortunately, the school caretaker was unable to distinguish between woodworm and pinholes so—ah . . ." Mr Pemberton-Oakes smiled knowingly to indicate that he, personally, would never have made so elementary a mistake. "So there is really no need for me to waste any more of your valuable time."

But Mr Marriott was not to be put off so easily. Having driven forty-five miles in quest of woodworm, he was not going to drive forty-five miles back again without giving the roof timbers a thorough inspection.

"I'll just have a look, now I'm here," he said. "Better be safe than sorry, I always say."

"Well, if you *insist*, of course . . ." Outwardly polite, but inwardly resentful of this time-wasting procedure, Mr Pemberton-Oakes escorted his visitor out into the corridor. Here they met Mr Carter returning to his room after entrusting Venables with the job of handing out the afternoon post.

"Ah, Carter! If you are going upstairs, I wonder if you would be kind enough to show Mr Marriott to the top floor," the headmaster said. "He's anxious to assure himself that the attics are, indeed, free from any infestation."

"Certainly," Mr Carter agreed. "I'd better find Robinson first, though. He's the only one with a key, I believe."

"Not the *only* one," Mr Pemberton-Oakes corrected with a wan smile. "From the facts that have recently come to light, it's quite obvious that Jennings has one, too!" He turned to the inspector of woodworm. "Mr Carter will show you round, Mr Marriott."

"Right!" Grasping a powerful torch in one hand and a magnifying glass in the other, the expert followed his guide up the stairs.

It was half an hour later when he returned to the ground floor and found his way back to the headmaster's study.

"Just as well I had a look round up top, Mr Pemberton-Oakes," he said briskly, setting his torch down on the headmaster's desk. "Fair riddled with worm, some of those roof timbers."

The headmaster looked at him in surprise. "But surely—that beam with the name on. I have definite proof that the damage was caused by drawing-pins."

"Oh, the beam's all right. Sound as a bell," the expert agreed. "But it won't be much longer if something isn't done about it. It was when I got up a bit higher, right into the roof, that I found the real trouble. And what's more, you've got a fair bit of worm in some of those other rooms on the top floor, too."

Mr Pemberton-Oakes' expression changed from surprise to concern. "You mean it's going to be an expensive matter to have it put right?"

The expert pursed his lips. "Not if you have it done soon, before it spreads much further," he conceded. "On the other hand, if you leave it to get worse you'll end up with the whole roof falling in on top of you one of these fine days!"

The headmaster was thoughtful as he walked back to his study after seeing Mr Marriott off in his car. He had arranged for the woodworm to be treated in a few weeks' time when the school would have broken up for the summer holidays. By taking measures now he would be spared a great deal of expense—not to mention the risk of physical danger—later on.

It was odd, he thought, that no one had noticed the infested rafters before. But why should they, when nobody ever went up to the attics—*except Jennings, of course!*

Mr Pemberton-Oakes frowned as he lowered himself into his swivel-chair. If it wasn't for Jennings they would never have discovered the woodworm until it was too late. It was hardly fair, he thought, to punish a boy who had saved the school a considerable amount of money and, in Mr Marriott's words, prevented the whole roof falling in on top of them one of these fine days!

"Well, Jennings," the headmaster proceeded as the boy stood staring at him in amazement from the other side of the desk. "I had, as you know, intended to punish you for breaking bounds and damaging school property. However, certain facts have come to light as a result of your—ah—little escapade in the attic, and as a result I have decided to say no more about your—ah—breach of school rules."

"You mean—no punishment, sir?"

"No, Jennings; there will be no punishment. Indeed your prank proved to be a blessing in disguise for which we all have reason to be grateful." The headmaster stretched his indulgent smile a further couple of millimetres. "That's all then, Jennings. You may run along, now."

"Thank you, sir. Thank you very much, sir."

"Er—one moment." Mr Pemberton-Oakes' raised finger stopped the boy as he turned to go. "You may be unaware of the fact that you have a streak of some substance—it may well be creosote or bicycle oil from the look of it—smeared down your left cheek."

Jennings' hand shot up to his face. "Sorry, sir. It's probably chocolate. Darbishire gave me a bit after tea and it was rather runny and . . ." He groped for his handkerchief, tugging it from his blazer pocket with a clumsy jerk. As it came clear, Johnny Gray's letter, caught in the folds, shot into the air and landed on the far side of the leather-topped desk.

The headmaster was about to pass it back without comment when he caught a glimpse of the printed heading where the sheet had been rumpled out of its folds in Jennings' pocket.

"*Dunhambury and District Gazette?*" he murmured inquiringly. "Since when have you been in correspondence with the local paper?" He unfolded the letter, curious to know what lay within.

Jennings' heart missed a beat and he became tense with apprehension. Having just been pardoned for one breach of school rules (and he still didn't know the reason why), it would be a cruel blow of fate if he was now taken to task on another, more serious one! He could have kicked himself for so clumsily revealing Mr Gray's letter. All that successful planning: all that painstaking subterfuge—and now this!

Mr Pemberton-Oakes read the letter through to the end and said, "I don't understand. What is all this about a fire, and your name being in the paper?"

Jennings took a deep breath. "Well, sir, it was when I was coming back from the dentist's last Thursday week. A lady asked me to telephone for the fire brigade and I did. And then this reporter, Mr Gray, that is, came up and said he'd put it in the paper, only he didn't."

"Did you mention this to anybody when you got back to school?"

"Only Darbishire and Atkinson and boys like that, sir," Jennings replied. "I—er—I didn't think there was any point in telling any of the masters."

The headmaster accepted the explanation with a nod. Unaware of the boy's unauthorised bus journey to East Brinkington and his adventures afoot and awheel in and around the parish of Birchingdean, Mr Pemberton-Oakes assumed that the fire had occurred at some point in Dunhambury between the dentist's surgery and the Linbury bus stop. In such circumstances he considered the boy had behaved in a highly commendable manner.

"That was a very public-spirited action, Jennings. I congratulate you," he said. "I trust you were not too disappointed that an account of the fire was not, after all, included in the paper as you had anticipated?"

"Oh, no, sir. I wasn't disappointed. In fact, I was rather . . ." He stopped just in time. To reveal how thankful he really was at the omission might have roused the headmaster's suspicions all over again. "Well, sir, perhaps I'd better go and—er—" He picked up his letter and stood awaiting permission to withdraw.

"Off you go, then," Mr Pemberton-Oakes said in kindly tones. "Well done, Jennings! Your conduct in summoning the fire brigade, and your modesty in not drawing attention to the incident is well worthy of the traditions of—ah—service and humility that we endeavour to instil into our boys at Linbury Court!"

The words sounded a trifle pompous (even for a headmaster), but Jennings listened with pride and relief. Provided that no more details were allowed to leak out, he could claim to have weathered the storm with flags flying.

"Thank you, sir. Thank you, very *much*, sir. Thank you, very much, *indeed*, sir," he said.

He strode from the room glowing in the aura of service and humility which he could almost feel floating a few inches above his head in the shape of a halo.

Chapter 14

Bird on the Wing

There was an unofficial, single-wicket Test Match in progress when Jennings came out on to the playing field after leaving the headmaster's study.

West Indies (represented by Venables and Darbishire) had just established a new record by scoring only seven runs (four of them wides) as their first innings total, and were just about to take the field in an endeavour to dismiss Australia (Temple and Atkinson) for an even lower score, if possible.

The match came to a standstill as Jennings appeared and both teams went hurrying towards him agog with curiosity to hear the spine-chilling details of his encounter with Mr Pemberton-Oakes. At the same time they tried to keep their faces grave and their brows creased in frowns of sympathy. The strain upon their facial muscles was considerable!

"So you're still alive, then!" Temple greeted him. "We thought there'd be nothing left except a tin of cat's food by the time the Archbeako had finished orbiting."

"Bad luck, Jen! It was worrying about what was happening to you that made me get bowled first ball," Darbishire sympathised.

They peered at him, hoping to detect marks of suffering and anguish upon his features and felt vaguely cheated at finding none. In fact, Jennings appeared to be looking more than usually pleased with himself.

"Well, go on—what happened?" Venables urged. "How many different sorts of punishment did you get?"

"I didn't get any. He said I was a blessing in disguise."

"Disguised as what?" Temple demanded suspiciously.

"I don't know. I didn't quite understand that bit, because actually I wasn't disguised as anything," Jennings assured him. "Of course, if I'd gone foxing up to the attic in a false beard and dark glasses I should have . . ."

"Never mind the blessed disguise, what did he actually say?" Atkinson wanted to know.

"He said he was grateful."

"He said *what*!" The audience of four exchanged incredulous glances. Was Jennings making fun of them, they wondered? Or had the headmaster gone out of his mind? The latter alternative seemed the more likely theory as Mr Pemberton-Oakes was thought to be at least forty-five and, at that advanced age, might well be the victim of senile decay.

"Yes, honestly," Jennings persisted, and his tone was so convincing that it banished their doubts. "And later on when he found out I'd put through that fire call . . ."

"He knew that too?" Darbishire gasped in dismay.

"Yes, but that was my fault. I dropped Mr Gray's letter on his desk and he read it."

"But he *must* have punished you for that," Darbishire squawked in disbelief. "Going for bus rides all round the county when you were supposed to be at the dentist's! To say nothing of . . ."

"He didn't know *everything* that happened," Jennings pointed out. "But because I didn't go about boasting and telling everyone, he said I was an example of—of—well, some old flannel-footed gobbledeygook—I can't remember what, but it meant I was a credit to the school."

This was unbelievable! This was a world of fantasy in which reason had no place! There was a short silence while they strove to adjust their minds to these new standards of adult behaviour. Then Temple said, "Well, that proves it. I've been thinking for some time that the Archbeako was going round the bend, and now we know. It was probably listening to old Jen confessing to the worst list of crimes since the Black Hole of Calcutta that brought on the brainstorm."

The cricketers wandered away to resume their interrupted Test Match, but Jennings was in no mood to join them. In spite of his lucky escapes he was worried: for now that news of his trespassing on the top floor had come to the ears of the staff, he could not run the risk of paying further visits to the tank attic.

So what about Swing-Wing? Until that morning the bird's catering requirements had been looked after by one of the three pigeon-fanciers creeping up the back stairs with a portion of the mixed seeds and corn which Mrs

Hackett had been continuing to buy for them from the village stores. Now, the bird would have to fend for itself: and though this would not involve any real hardship, Jennings felt unhappy in his mind at the idea of breaking the relationship so abruptly. Swing-Wing was his special responsibility. There was a bond between them, and to abandon him now would be a betrayal of the care and protection which the pigeon had come to expect.

Besides, he was still hoping to return the bird to its owner, Jennings reminded himself. The fact that his first attempt had been a failure was no reason to give up trying.

He wished now that he had told the headmaster more about his secret pet; but Mr Pemberton-Oakes had shot off at a tangent about starlings on telephone wires when the subject was mentioned, and would almost certainly have disapproved of the project, anyway.

Jennings turned his back on the Test Match (in which both teams were now arguing about a lost ball) and stood for some while looking up at the attic window where Swing-Wing, having just emerged from beneath the eaves, was pacing the sill waiting for his evening meal.

Poor old pigeon, Jennings thought! He wouldn't understand why they had abandoned him. He'd never know why his food supply was suddenly cut off. He might even pine away and . . .

"I shouldn't worry, Jennings. I don't think he'll starve!"

The deep, adult voice sounding just behind him made the boy leap with shock. Wheeling round, he glanced up to see Mr Carter standing a few feet away, smiling and watching him with a look of understanding.

"Oh, sir! You made me jump. I didn't hear you coming

sir," Jennings exclaimed. A thought struck him and he said in puzzled wonder, "But how did you know what I was thinking about?"

"I've got eyes," said Mr Carter. "Seeing you staring so forlornly at your old friend the pigeon whom you may not be able to visit so readily in future . . ."

So Mr Carter *knew*! Jennings was astounded. "How—how did you find out, sir?"

"I *didn't* find out—until this afternoon; otherwise I should have done something about it before," Mr Carter told him. "But after lunch today it so happened that I took a visitor up to the attic, and while he prowled around with a torch and a magnifying glass I made friends with your bird on the window-sill." His smile broadened as he went on, "Judging by the well-defined marks made by the bird's water-pot, to say nothing of the remains of wheat and millet seeds strewn about the sill, it was obvious that well-organised catering arrangements had been going on for some time."

"Well, yes, sir, that's quite right, sir," Jennings confessed.

"I don't know who else was engaged in the operation, but your name up on the beam seemed to imply who was in charge," Mr Carter observed pleasantly. "The thing that beats me is why you didn't come and ask permission to do all this openly, instead of getting everything tangled up by breaking school rules left right and centre."

Jennings looked surprised. Surely, the answer was obvious! "Because the attics are out of bounds, sir!"

Mr Carter tut-tutted patiently. "The object of putting the attics out of bounds is to stop boys playing about up there when they have no reason to do so," he explained. "If they need to visit them for some good purpose, any master could give permission. It doesn't need an Act of Parliament, you know!"

"Oh, I see, sir. I didn't realise."

Mr Carter was the duty master that evening and had been making a tour of the playing fields when he had stopped to speak to Jennings. Now, he continued on his round taking the boy with him; and as they made their way about the grounds Jennings told him about Swing-Wing: how they had secretly obtained his provisions from the village stores; how they had been hoping to return him to his owner, but were frustrated by lack of information; how they would have carried out the whole project openly but for the thought that permission to do so would have been refused.

Mr Carter listened with a sympathetic ear. He was that sort of man. You could tell him anything and he would understand.

The dormitory bell was ringing by the time they had strolled round the playing fields together, and Jennings went off to join his colleagues who were making their way indoors.

"You should have come and watched our Test Match," Temple said to him as they reached the dormitory. "It was brilliant. Atki hit the ball into the nettles and old Ven and Darbi got so stung trying to find it that they forgot to shout *lost ball* and we made seventeen runs off one hit."

Jennings was barely interested in this unusual feat. "It's going to be all right about Swing-Wing," he announced when all his friends had assembled. "Mr Carter's going to find out who the owner is, so we can send him home; and what's more, he's going to ask the Head if we can go on looking after him until we know where to send him back to."

The announcement was received with enthusiasm. Only Atkinson had a slight criticism to offer.

"Well, I hope to goodness Sir's a bit better at finding out where he lives than you, Jennings," he said. "Otherwise, he'll still be roosting outside the window when we're all queueing up for our old-age pension."

As it happened, Mr Carter's research produced such speedy results that even Atkinson had no cause to complain. He came into the dining-hall during the boys' tea the following afternoon and stopped at the third-form table.

"I've just been writing to a man in the Midlands who keeps a register of pigeons' ring numbers," he told them. "With luck we'll know who your feathered friend belongs to in a few days' time."

Jennings looked at the master in mild surprise. It was less than twenty-four hours since Mr Carter had expressed his willingness to help.

"But how did you know who to write to, sir?" he demanded. "We went to an awful lot of trouble and then we didn't find out in the end."

Mr Carter smiled. "A simple deduction. You told me that Mrs Hackett had been getting the pigeon mixture from Linbury Stores. That suggested that they had other customers who kept homing birds, so I went in and asked them."

"Oh, I see . . . And had they, sir?"

"Yes. They put me on to Mr Lumley who keeps that little café in the village. You may remember it has a pigeon loft in the garden. He told me whom to get in touch with."

Jennings frowned at his beetroot salad in self-reproach. He had known from the start where Mrs Hackett bought the pigeon mixture! Why hadn't *he* thought of making inquiries at the village stop instead of traipsing half round the county to no purpose?

Less than a week later they had the information they needed. The letter arrived at breakfast time on Friday and Mr Carter passed on the news as soon as the meal was over.

"The owner of the bird with the ring number N 720 NU 67 is a Mr J. Saltmarsh of Old Mill Farm, near Swaffham, Norfolk," he announced to the group of pigeon-fanciers who were waiting for him outside the dining-hall. "You'd better write a letter to Mr Saltmarsh, Jennings, and see it gets posted today."

"Yes, sir, rather sir," Jennings agreed. "Shall I tell him we're sending it back in Temple's fishing basket?"

The owner of the receptacle was standing nearby and was only too pleased to co-operate. "You do that, Jen. I'll give it a good spring-clean at break and get it all lined with wood shavings and stuff."

"He'll want some drinking-water, too, if he's going all that way," Atkinson said thoughtfully. "I wonder if I could make an unspillable drinking trough out of a school inkwell or something."

Everybody seemed anxious to help in speeding Swing-Wing's departure. Mr Carter telephoned the railway station, Darbishire wrote labels in large block capitals,

Venables pierced larger air holes in the lid of the basket, and Binns and Blotwell, with the help of a school atlas, worked out the mileage of the journey and where the bird would have to change trains.

Jennings, meanwhile, was poring over his writing pad. The first draft of his letter read:

Dear Mr Saltmarsh,

I expect you will be pleased to hear that your racing pigeon No. N 720 NU 67 whom I expect you fear is lost for ever and will not see again is fit and well as I expect you will be pleased to hear. He has been on our window-sill for about five weeks as you will be surprised to learn.

We tried to send him back before, but he flew home (ie viz back to school) and we did not know your address until Mr Carter found out which we should never have done by ourselves if I had not put my name on the beam in drawing pins so it really was a Blessing in Disguise.

We are sending him back (by kind permission of C. A. Temple) under separate cover in a fishing basket by train, please return the basket and he will get there on Saturday, July 15 at 21.45 hours (ie tomorrow) so please meet him at the station and acknowledge receipt of same.

Must stop now as am running out of ink. I beg to remain your obedient servant.

Yours sincerely,
(Singed) J. C. T. Jennings.

Mr Carter refused to pass this draft and Jennings was sent away with instructions to express his thoughts more clearly. At his third attempt he produced a letter which the master considered to be adequate.

"It's not perfect, but it'll have to do or you'll miss the post," Mr Carter told him when he looked through the letter after school. "I've arranged to take the pigeon to the station first thing tomorrow morning, so you'd better make sure he's ready to go."

"Yes, sir."

Jennings hurried down the hall and dropped the letter in the post box. It would arrive first thing on Saturday morning, he reckoned, so Mr Saltmarsh would have all day to prepare for his bird's homecoming.

Then he went in search of his fellow fanciers whom he found in the common-room putting the finishing touches to Swing-Wing's travelling basket.

"I'm just doing an extra label to tie on the outside," Darbishire explained, "telling the station-master to look after him and give him his supper if Mr Saltmarsh turns up late."

This done, the three boys took the basket up to the top floor. They clattered up the stairs chatting at the tops of their voices, enjoying the novelty of "trespassing" with permission.

"We'll put him in his basket straight away and let him spend the night there," Jennings announced. "Then we won't have to keep Sir waiting, trying to catch him in the morning."

There was no need for Jennings to use his key, for the

attic was now left unlocked. Once inside, he opened the window wide and beckoned Swing-Wing out from his retreat under the eaves. As usual, the bird approached, strutting along the sill in search of food, and as it reached the open window Jennings picked it up gently, placed it in the basket and shut down the lid.

"Good-bye, Swing-Wing," he called softly through the wicker-work. "You're going home tomorrow."

"Lucky old him! We've got the best part of a fortnight to wait before *our* last night of term," Atkinson grumbled. He finished pouring a portion of corn from a packet into an empty tobacco tin. "Hey, what about his supper, Jen? You can't bed him down for the night if he's still hungry."

Jennings had forgotten the bird's rations. "Bung it over then, and I'll give it to him in his basket," he said.

He took the little tin of food in one hand while with the other he threw back the lid.

The result was unexpected. As the lid rose, so did the bird! With a flutter of wings it flew straight out of the basket, veered through the wide-open window and out into the evening sunshine.

It all happened so quickly that the boys were left helpless and gasping in the wake of the fluttering wings. Indeed, Darbishire, who had turned round for a moment to look at Mr Wilkins' handiwork on the beam, wasn't aware that anything was wrong until the horrified squawks of Jennings and Atkinson sent him rushing to the window. He arrived just in time to see a graceful swirl of tail feathers soaring high over the cricket pavilion and growing smaller every moment.

"You great, crazy bazooka, Jennings!" Atkinson stormed when the power of speech returned. "What did you want to take the lid off for?"

"Well, how was I to know he was going to shoot off like that?" Jennings defended himself.

"Of *course* you should have known. It's exactly what happened last time, isn't it!"

Jennings had no excuse to offer. It was all his fault, he admitted to himself, for the incident was similar in many respects to Swing-Wing's escape from his container in Mrs Goodman's garden at East Brinkington.

"It's because he's been trained as a racing bird—that's what caused it," he said in an attempt to mitigate his lapse. "They're trained to be quick off the mark as soon as the basket is opened and—well, I just didn't think."

Atkinson snorted. "It's sabotage, if you ask me. He's only been put in the basket twice since we've had him, and both times you had to go and take the lid off."

Darbishire did his best to patch up the quarrel. "Perhaps he's coming back," he suggested hopefully. "After all he goes for a fly round the playing fields several times a day and he always comes back for his food." He strained his eyes to the north-east in the direction the bird had taken, but by now Swing-Wing was out of sight behind the trees.

"He doesn't zoom off like a moon rocket when he's coming back for his supper," Atkinson argued. "He just flops about in the trees like a toy balloon and stops to scratch his head every few yards."

For a while they stood at the window and waited, but there was no sign of the bird returning and they knew in their hearts that Swing-Wing had gone for good. Perhaps it was the close confines of the travelling basket that had aroused his racing instincts to be off and away; perhaps he had suddenly grown tired of roosting under the eaves; whatever the reason, he had departed as suddenly as he had arrived, and with as little formality.

Darbishire pulled a face and said, "That's that, then! I suppose we'd better go and tell Mr Carter to cancel the royal train."

Jennings agreed with a nod. "I only wish to goodness he'd had the decency to belt off half an hour ago."

"Why?" demanded Atkinson. "If he was going anyway, I can't see that half an hour makes any difference."

"It makes a really important difference, I'd have you know," Jennings replied as he shut the window and turned to leave the room. "Half an hour ago I hadn't posted that letter to Mr Saltmarsh. A proper sort of Charlie I'm going to look when he gets the letter and then finds there's no pigeon to go with it."

Chapter 15

Outlook Unsettled

They never saw Swing-Wing again; and for some days there was no reply to Jennings' letter, posted so needlessly just before the bird's departure. But on the following Friday, when less than a week remained before the school broke up for the holidays, Jennings received a parcel bearing a Norfolk post-mark.

It was a flat, rectangular parcel—a book by the shape of it—and he could hardly wait till the end of breakfast to see what the package contained. As soon as he was clear of the dining-hall he rushed upstairs to the common-room where, surrounded by a group of interested spectators, he cut the string and tore off the wrapping.

Inside was a book, as expected, covered with a coloured wrapper depicting a group of birds in flight. There was also a letter, so he picked it up and read it aloud.

Dear J. C. T. Jennings,

I was delighted to receive your letter last Saturday and to learn that my pigeon, missing since the middle of June, was safe and well. The bird strayed during a training flight and I was concerned in case it had come to any harm.

However, your letter reassured me; and with the news that you were despatching the bird by rail I went to the station to meet the train...

No pigeon! And again I feared that it was lost, but to my delight it turned up at my loft the next morning, having made the journey on the wing. Considering the bird has been out of training for some weeks it looks remarkably fit—a tribute to the way you and your friends have been looking after it. Many thanks for all your care and attention.

As a small tribute I am enclosing a book which I wrote a few years ago on a subject which has been of interest to me ever since I was about the age that I imagine you to be now.

I hope you (and your friends) like the book. And if it inspires you to take a closer look at the feathered world, I trust that what you will find there will give you as much pleasure over the years as it has given me.

Yours sincerely,

John D. Saltmarsh.

There was a respectful silence as Jennings read the letter. Then, everybody wanted to see the book.

"Hey, stand back!" Jennings protested as the crowd

surged forward and pinned him against the lockers. "I haven't even got room to open it with you mob shoving like a rugger scrum."

In self-defence he pushed the book up his sweater and forced his way out of the room in search of privacy. Only Darbishire and Atkinson were allowed to accompany him, and together the three went down to the basement and sat on a row of tuck-boxes to inspect the gift in peace and comfort.

It was a large book, well illustrated with photographs, and even before they had flicked through the pages they learned something about the author from a paragraph on the inside flap of the dust jacket.

J. D. Saltmarsh, it appeared, as well as being a show judge and an experienced breeder of pigeons was also an authority on many sorts of wildfowl. He had made a bird sanctuary on some marshland near his home and much of his book was devoted to describing his bird-watching activities.

Jennings turned over the flyleaf, and as his eye fell upon the title page he felt a glow of pleasure and pride. Written in the same neat handwriting which characterised the ornithologist's letter was the inscription:

Signed by the author for J. C. T. Jennings and his friends at Linbury Court School—John D. Saltmarsh —With many thanks for a service rendered.

"Wow! How about that, then!" Jennings exclaimed, jabbing the inscription with a sticky forefinger. "This makes it our very own special private possession. I've never had a book signed by the author, before."

"Well, now you've got one you needn't blot it all out," Atkinson said in rebuke. "Nobody will be able to read ye famous signature by the time you've finished smearing your dirty great paws all over it."

"I'll be careful," Jennings agreed. "I'm going to wash my hands and write and thank Mr Saltmarsh, and then I'm going to get my nose stuck in the book till I've finished it."

"Bags after you," Darbishire put in quickly.

"And me next, after Darbishire," said Atkinson. "I bet you what you like everyone will start queueing up to borrow it when they see what a good book it is."

It was, in Jennings' phrase, a good time to get one's nose stuck in a book, for not only was the weekend before them, but, with the end of term so close at hand masters would sometimes decide to devote a lesson to silent reading while they busied themselves with writing reports. Thus it was that during the next few days Jennings, Darbishire and Atkinson all read the book themselves and still had time to pass it on to several of their friends.

The result was a sudden, passionate wave of interest in ornithology which swept through Form Three like a prairie fire. All at once everybody became a birdlover, everybody was eager to take up this fascinating hobby. *Birds in Their Habitat* by J. D. Saltmarsh was a work that ranged freely over the whole field of ornithology and every chapter stirred the imagination of one or more of these avid readers.

For example, the section on pigeons inspired Atkinson and Venables with the determination to convert a disused potting-shed in the headmaster's garden into a well-equipped loft for racing birds.

"We could get permish from Mr Carter and build up a

team of international racers,' Atkinson announced to Form Three table at lunch on Monday. "Then, instead of just playing Bracebridge School at cricket or football we could challenge them to pigeon races, too. Of course, *they'd* have to keep pigeons as well," he went on, dismissing the obstacles involved with a wave of his fork, "but it'd be fantastically exciting, wouldn't it!"

Darbishire's enthusiasm was fired by the section on fantail pigeons, and he decided there and then to become a world-famous authority on the subject when he grew up. Already, as he put the book down, he could picture in his mind's eye the scene in the foyer of the Natural History Museum as zoologists from every part of the globe craned forward to catch a glimpse of the tall, intellectual-looking figure with the scholarly stoop who was entering through the main doors.

"Know who that is?" they were saying to one another in a dozen different languages. "That's Professor C. E. J. Darbishire, the eminent expert. He knows so much about fantail pigeons that he's forgotten more about them than most people could ever hope to learn."

Indeed, Darbishire was so eager to start his life's work that after cricket on Tuesday he prevailed upon Jennings to help him construct a fantail loft for use at some unspecified time in the future.

Robinson had thrown a rack of old shoe-lockers on the rubbish heap pending an end-of-term bonfire, and as Darbishire decided that it was just the right shape for his needs, he and Jennings salvaged the battered object and set to work to turn a receptacle for juvenile footwear into a home fit for fantails to live in.

Mr Wilkins strolled by as they were prising out rusty

nails with a dessert fork borrowed from the cutlery drawer in the dining-hall.

"What in the name of thunder are you boys playing at?" he demanded.

"Building a fantail dovecote, sir," Darbishire answered proudly.

The master stared at them in bewilderment. "But you haven't *got* any fantails, you silly little boy."

"No, sir, I know we haven't. But building a cote for them is the next best thing. We're—sort of—making it for its own sake, as you might say."

This made no sense to Mr Wilkins, so Jennings said, "We shall probably have some one day, sir, when our wildfowl sanctuary gets going."

"Your *what*?"

"Birds' camp site, sir. Didn't you know? We're planning to set one up behind the pond." He pointed towards the far end of the grounds where a copse of trees surrounded a marshy pool. "We're planning to do it properly with anti-fox barriers and all that sort of thing. *If* we can get permission, that is."

"Well, *I'm* not giving anyone permission for any fantastic tomfoolery of that sort," Mr Wilkins replied curtly. "Take those shoelockers back where you found them— *and* that fork—and go and get yourselves cleaned up for tea."

But Mr Wilkins could do little to stem the tide of enthusiasm which, for the moment, had fired the imagination of Jennings and his bird-loving comrades in Form Three. As the master strode round the playing field on his tour of duty, he came across one instance after another of how quickly the craze had taken root.

Venables and Temple, who would normally have been playing French cricket, were crouching in the shrubbery peering up into the branches of an elder tree. Venables was holding a small toy telescope to his eye, and as the master came within earshot he was saying, "M'yes, it *could* be a Sedge-Warbler, I suppose. It's definitely not a Red-backed Shrike." He spoke in the confident tone of an expert giving a considered opinion.

"I thought perhaps it was a Blue-headed Wagtail," Temple hazarded. "Either that or a Cirl-Bunting."

At that moment the bird flew out of the shrubbery straight across Mr Wilkins' line of vision. One glance was enough to identify it as a female blackbird.

Tut! Silly little boys, he thought as he passed on. They couldn't have told a sparrow from a kingfisher!

Near the cricket pavilion he came across Bromwich stalking a lapwing with his camera, and down by the pond he found Thompson joining up rusty pieces of wire netting as part of Jennings' plan to render the bird sanctuary proof against the depredations of foxes. Wherever he went, wherever he looked, the duty master was confronted with bird-studying activities of one sort or another.

When he got back to the playground, Henri Dufour was, for some inexplicable reason, counting the number of starlings perching on the telephone wire and entering the results in a notebook.

Mr Wilkins could see no purpose in this pointless

census. "Why are you doing that?" he asked in the slow, deliberate tones in which he always addressed the French boy. "The birds will have flown away before you have finished counting them."

Henri smiled and replied in his best English, "The birds were there tomorrow, so I think they will be here yesterday, also. No?"

Mr Wilkins gave it up, and moved on across the playground. As he turned the corner by the gymnasium the stillness of the afternoon was suddenly shattered by an eerie, staccato laugh which grated unpleasantly on the ear ... It was Binns and Blotwell practising the call of the lesser-spotted woodpecker.

By the time he arrived back in the staff room Mr Wilkins was suffering from an overdose of ornithology. In his opinion the current project was playing havoc with the smooth-running routine of Linbury Court School.

"You certainly started something when you got Jennings to write to that pigeon-fancier," he complained to Mr Carter as he settled himself down in an armchair. "That wretched book has made them so keen that they're even planning to set up a bird sanctuary in the school grounds, if you please."

Mr Carter was quite unperturbed. "I rather thought they'd want to do something like that. Especially Jennings—he never knows when to stop."

"But it's ridiculous! We shall have to clamp down on it before it gets completely out of hand." Mr Wilkins formed a mental picture of the chaos to come and, giving his imagination free rein, he declaimed, "Before we know what's happening we'll have the whole lot escaping and running riot all over the grounds. Cormorants on the cricket pitch, swans in the swimming bath, buzzards in the bicycle shed, penguins in the pavilion . . ."

"Flamingoes on the fire escape and ravens on the writing desks," Mr Carter murmured, but Mr Wilkins was not listening. Warming to his theme he went on:

"Think of it, Carter, if this ridiculous craze isn't nipped in the bud we shall have the whole school turned into a vast, flapping maelstrom of feathered songsters, cawing and croaking from dawn till dusk."

He broke off and frowned when he saw that his colleague was looking at him with quiet amusement. "It's no laughing matter, Carter. When once that boy Jennings gets an idea in his head anything *can* happen—and quite a lot of things *do*!"

Still smiling, Mr Carter filled his pipe. "You seem to have forgotten, Wilkins, that in two days from now they will all—including Jennings—be going home for the holidays."

"Thank goodness for that," Mr Wilkins said fervently.

"In seven weeks' time they'll be back again, bursting at the seams with some new interest which has just taken their fancy. Nobody knows what it will be, but I can tell you this, Wilkins—it won't be feathered songsters. Birds will have had their innings by then."

The tea-bell rang and Mr Wilkins rose and glanced out of the window at the swarms of bird-lovers pouring into the building for the evening meal. In the forefront was Jennings, and at the sight of him, Mr Wilkins' forebodings returned.

"Are you *sure* they will have forgotten all about it by next term?" he asked doubtfully.

Mr Carter nodded. "Quite sure!"

And, as usual, Mr Carter proved to be right!